SHUKÁRA
SHADOWS OF THE HEART

SCOTT DEVAUGHN

SHUKARA PUBLISHING

CONTENTS

CHAPTER 1: ARRIVAL

Scene 1: Descent into Uncertainty

Shukára's knuckles reddened, gripping her harness as the cargo plane bucked, and its metal groaned. Towering crates collided against their restraints. Lightning fractured the sky in impossible shades of violet and green, painting her face in unusual hues. Her pulse quickened, not from the otherworldly storm that came out of nowhere; but because somewhere below, lay answers about Quin. Six months since her twin had vanished. Six months too long.

"Something's coming, sis," he'd said, staring at his pendant identical to hers. "Reality isn't what we thought." She'd laughed then, teased him for being dramatic. Now, months since his disappearance, those words haunted her.

The pendant warmed against her skin as another bolt of unnatural lightning split the sky. This time, she wouldn't ignore the signs.

The shaking grew ferocious as she held on. Crates rattled, and the military metal beast whined under the strain. Thunder boomed. The colored storm lit Shukára's face again, yet fear held no place in her expression. Her mind locked onto one goal: discovering what happened to Quin.

Through the small window, she watched the roiling clouds thin and part, just as quickly as the odd storm had appeared only moments before, revealing the mist-shrouded forest below. The covert Forward Operating Base Epsilon sprawled like a metallic fortress nestled amidst the rugged terrain. Its steel and glass structures gleaming under the muted sunlight—the likely last place her brother operated.

Her fingers wrapped around a worn pendant, sitting where her dog tag would rest if not headed to a covert base. The pendant, Kara's most beloved connection to Quin, carried intricate designs now dulled by her anxious touch.

The steady whine of her transport filled the air, a constant backdrop to her racing thoughts. Her heartbeat quickened as she glanced down.

On the final descent, the intercom crackled to life. "Prepare for landing," a voice barked.

Shukára took a deep breath, her eyes never leaving the base growing larger beneath her. She whispered, "I'm coming for you, Quin."

Scene 2: Covert Forward Operating Base Epsilon

The plane landed with a jolt. The ramp lowered with a mechanical hiss, revealing a hive of activity on the tarmac. Drones buzzed overhead like automated bees. Holographic displays flickered with streams of data, and soldiers moved with practiced precision, intermingled with ground-based hovercraft.

She stepped off the plane into the crisp mountain air, tinged with the scent of ozone from the high-tech equipment. Adjusting the strap of her duffel bag, she put her senses on high alert.

"First time at Epsilon?" a voice called out.

She turned to see a tall man approaching, his uniform bearing the insignia of a communications officer. His warm brown eyes and big smile offered an unexpected cheerful welcome in this unfamiliar place.

"Specialist Shukára Vallian," extending her hand.

"Specialist Marcus Thompson," shaking hands. "Welcome to the cutting edge."

Shukára offered a small smile. "Thank you. Call me Kara, and..." She looked around with wonder.

Marcus chuckled. "Yes, it's impressive if you like steel and secrets. Let me help you get settled."

As they walked, Marcus glanced at the pendant around her neck. "That's an interesting piece."

Her hand moved, curling around it. "Family heirloom," with a guarded smile, unsure of how much to reveal.

He nodded. "Seems like it has a story."

"Don't we all?" she gave a hint of a smile.

Marcus met her eyes, curiosity flickering. "Fair enough. Let's get you oriented. There's a lot to see, and," he lowered his voice, "a lot to learn about how things work around here."

Scene 3: Entering the Base with Marcus

Shukára's eyes widened as they moved through sleek corridors lined with transparent panels showcasing exotic plants glowing with bioluminescence. Robotic arms whirred behind glass barriers, assembling complex devices. Nature and science had found a delicate balance within these walls.

"Quite the place," Kara taking it all in.

Marcus leaned in. "Epsilon prides itself on being ahead of the curve. Just know that not everything is as it seems."

She glanced at him. "Meaning?"

He offered a casual shrug, but his expression remained serious. "Just keep your eyes open."

Kara raised an eyebrow.

They passed a group of soldiers who eyed them with indifference. Kara noticed that despite the advanced technology, they lacked advanced camaraderie; and they had an undercurrent of tension threading through the base.

"I appreciate the heads-up."

They passed a group of scientists huddled around a holographic display, their whispers creating a buzz of energy. Kara caught fragments of their conversation—something about "quantum entanglement" and "cross-dimensional symmetry."

Marcus gave her a reassuring smile. "Anytime, we're all on the same team."

She nodded, yet an unsettled feeling lingered—alliances here seemed more complicated than they appeared.

Kara noticed the subtle signs of surveillance—the lenses hidden in the walls, the way the lighting adjusted as they moved, as if tracking them. A chill ran down her spine.

Scene 4: Orientation with Captain Samantha Reed

"Orientation is this way." Marcus pointed down a corridor lined with seamless glass doors. "I'll see you afterward?"

"Sure," she agreed. "Thanks for the warm welcome."

He flashed her a reassuring smile. "Anytime, Kara."

As she made her way to Briefing Room Alpha, Kara could sense the eyes of hidden surveillance upon her. Marcus's words echoed in her mind: that not everything is as it seems. The corridor seemed to stretch endlessly, the polished floors reflecting her image like a mirror.

The briefing room spread out as a vast auditorium with tiered seating and a domed ceiling that projected a 360-degree holographic display of the world.

New specialists filled the seats, their faces illuminated by the soft glow of holographic interfaces embedded in the desks. See-through screens displayed data streams and mission stats. The air hummed with the low buzz of advanced machinery and the murmur of hushed conversations.

Kara took a seat near the center, her senses on high alert. A woman stepped onto the platform—a commanding presence with sharp features, piercing blue steely eyes, and blonde hair pulled back into a tight bun.

"Welcome to Forward Operating Base Epsilon," her voice rang steady and authoritative. "I am Captain Samantha Reed. You are here because you are the best—handpicked for your skills and potential. Here, we don't just defend; we innovate. We push the boundaries of what's possible."

As Captain Reed spoke, the holographic display shifted to show images of advanced weaponry, stealth aircraft, and lab experiments. Kara's eyes narrowed as she glimpsed the words "Project Chimera" on a folder in a lab image.

Reed's gaze swept the room, as if surveilling for something, lingering for a moment on Kara's pendant. An icy wave rippled through Kara as their eyes met. Something in Reed's look—recognition? Suspicion? Kara knew one thing: Reed could not be underestimated.

Captain Reed held her gaze for a moment longer before addressing the group again. "Dismissed. Report to your assigned units at 0600."

Scene 5: First Glimpse of Zayn

As the briefing concluded, and personnel dispersed, Kara scanned the crowd. That's when she saw him.

He stood apart from the others, his presence magnetic. Intense silver-blue eyes, set in a stoic face, locked onto hers from across the room. For a moment, time stood still. Something about him—a mysterious aura—pulled her in.

Before Kara could blink, he vanished, slipping out of the room with fluid grace. She wondered if she'd imagined the entire encounter.

A knowing smirk from Marcus told her she hadn't. "I see you've noticed Zayn," his tone teasing. "He has that effect on people."

Kara felt an unfamiliar flush creep up her neck. "What! I was just—"

Marcus chuckled. "Of course. Anyway, he's one of the best here, but he keeps to himself and he is a little different."

Kara filed that information away. "Seems like there's a lot of 'different' around here."

Marcus laughed. "You have no idea. Shall we continue the tour?"

Scene 6: Touring the Base Facilities

They continued through the labyrinthine corridors, entering the advanced training facilities. The space buzzed with activity—soldiers sparring alone in holographic arenas, while others engaged in solo simulation pods.

"This is where the magic happens," Marcus gesturing around. "Innovative tech to enhance individual performance in every way."

Kara watched as a soldier moved with superhuman speed, assisted by a sleek exoskeleton suit. Robotic assistants monitored vitals and provided real-time coaching. "Faster, concentrate, focus!"

"This is awesome," she admitted, "and so... automated."

Marcus grinned. "You mean individualized and unwelcoming?"

Kara bemoaned, "Yes!"

Marcus nodded. "You would think that teamwork and our common bonds would be front and center."

Kara looked at Marcus. "Maybe we are the ones who change that!"

Marcus smiled. "Learn where the bathrooms are first."

They approached a section cordoned off by heavy security measures. Guards stood at attention, and the air seemed thicker.

"What's in there?" Kara asked.

Marcus glanced at the sealed doors. "Classified," he said, but his eyes betrayed a hint of concern.

"Another thing to keep my eyes open about?" she probed.

He met her gaze. "Just focus on your training. The rest will come in time."

Kara, not satisfied with the answer, moved on—for now.

Scene 7: Initial Assessment

The assessment center doors slid open to reveal a vast chamber filled with equipment that pulsed with innovative technology. Holographic interfaces shimmered in the air, and the floor seemed alive with light and energy.

"Time to see what you're made of," Marcus offering an encouraging smile.

Kara squared her shoulders. "Bring it on."

The first challenge started without warning. The chamber shuddered and reconfigured—walls sliding, floors rotating, ceilings dropping. Most candidates needed time to adjust, to find their bearings. Not Kara. She moved through the shifting space as if she'd memorized its patterns, each step precise, each turn timed. Her body flowed through gaps moments before they appeared.

Dr. Vasquez leaned forward, observing from the control room above, frowning at her displays. "This can't be right. She's anticipating the configurational changes before the computer initiates them."

The combat simulation activated next. Twelve holographic opponents materialized, their forms flickering with deadly intent. Kara's eyes narrowed, tracking their movements. A slight smirk crossed her face.

"The targeting matrix has a dead zone at 45 degrees," she said to herself before diving through what appeared to be solid light. The holograms stuttered, unable to track her. "And the AI telegraphs—left shoulder drops before every strike," as she took them out one by one.

Dr. Vasquez's fingers flew across her console. "The system can't keep up with her. These readings... they're virtually unprecedented."

The final test filled the chamber with streams of complex data, shifting and flowing like digital rivers. Kara moved through them, connecting patterns, solving puzzles that should have taken much longer to decode. Her hands moved through the holographic data with impossible precision, finding connections that shouldn't have been visible to the human eye.

Dr. Vasquez turned to Captain Reed, "I've seen this once before, in the contrac—"

Captain Reed held out her hand, directing Dr. Vasquez to stop. Captain Reed stood motionless, her eyes fixed on Kara's performance. Her fingers tightened on her tablet as numbers flashed across the screen.

"Her performance is as expected. Stop talking about The Contractor," Reed's posture portrayed deeper interest. "Keep monitoring." She highlighted a series of numbers that had Dr. Vasquez's eyes widening.

Below, Kara completed the final sequence, barely winded. The chamber powered down around her, returning to its original configuration. Her gaze remained sharp, alert—absorbing every detail, mapping every corner, every shadow.

She looked up toward the observation window, and for a moment, her gaze seemed to pierce straight through the one-way glass, meeting Reed's eyes as if the barrier didn't exist.

Reed nodded as if to say, "I see you too." Her expression remained neutral, but under her voice, she said, "I got you!"

Scene 8: Settling into Quarters and Late-Night Reflection

Exhausted but satisfied, Kara made her way to her assigned quarters. The room offered minimalist comfort, with a large window overlooking the dense forest surrounding the base.

She unpacked her belongings methodically, placing a framed baby photo of herself and Quin on the nightstand. The memory brought a pang of longing.

In the image, a faded snapshot from the night of their birth, an elderly woman in elaborate traditional garments, her silver hair adorned with ancient symbols, placed identical pendants around them. Her eyes held the wisdom of ages. Strange lights flickered in the photo's background—dismissed by her parents as "cheap film." Those lights matched the violet and green glow of the impossible storm on the plane earlier today. The realization sent a chill through her core.

"When all realms align, twin guardians will be born," the woman had proclaimed. "The realms' pendants will protect them until they are ready to protect those realms."

Her father had laughed, thanking the mysterious visitor while exchanging concerned looks with her mother. Yet for all their skepticism, neither parent ever suggested removing the pendants.

And as Kara and Quin grew, the pendants became as much a part of them as their twin bond. Somehow that story has always comforted Kara and even comforts her now in this cold place.

An alert chimed on her tablet. "Assessment results to be reviewed in the morning briefing."

She sighed, running a hand through her hair. The weight of the day settled on her, but her mind could not rest.

Stepping out onto the small balcony, she gazed at the moonlit landscape. The forest seemed to whisper secrets as shadows danced between the trees. Something about this place felt connected to that night, to the old woman's words about realms and guardians.

"I'm closer than ever," she murmured. "I'll find you."

A distant, ominous howl pierced the silence, raising the hairs on the back of her neck. The cry came from what sounded like an enormous wolf, yet it held something more—a call directed at Kara, urging caution, demanding vigilance.

She shook off the unease and returned inside, drawing the curtains. Sleep came fitfully, her dreams filled with indistinct figures and echoes of her brother's voice.

Scene 9: Unexpected Encounter with Zayn

Unable to rest, Kara wandered through the base's corridors, hoping to tire herself out. The halls lay silent, bathed in soft lighting that cast long shadows.

Turning a corner, she nearly collided with someone.

"Whoa!" she stumbled back.

A firm hand caught her arm, steadying her. "Easy there," a familiar voice said.

She looked up to see Zayn's silver-blue eyes gazing down upon her. Up close, she could see flecks of green in his irises.

"Sorry, I wasn't paying attention," recognizing an unfamiliar flush rise to her cheeks.

"No harm done," a faint smile tugging at his lips.

For a moment, neither of them moved. Kara noticed his hand still on her arm, the warmth of his touch.

She cleared her throat. "Couldn't sleep?"

He released her gently. "Something like that."

Her fingers fiddled with her pendant out of habit. Zayn's eyes followed the movement, a flicker of recognition crossing his face. His expression shifted from surprise to inquisitive warmth. "Interesting pendant."

"It's... important to me," she said.

He nodded. "You should be careful, wandering around at night."

Raising an eyebrow. "I can handle myself."

A hint of a smirk appeared. "I don't doubt it. Just be careful around here."

Tilting her head back. "You sound like Marcus."

"Maybe he has a point." He glanced down the corridor. "I should go."

Before she could respond, he turned and walked away, his light footsteps echoing until he disappeared around a corner.

Kara stared after him, more intrigued than ever. Something about Zayn pulled at her curiosity. And she couldn't shake the feeling he knew more than he let on.

Scene 10: Restless Dreams

Returning to her quarters, Kara drifted into a restless sleep. Vivid dreams consumed her—a labyrinth of corridors leading nowhere, shadowy figures vanishing as she approached, and always the distant call of her brother.

"Quin!" she called out, but her voice echoed back, unanswered.

The eerie howl she'd heard earlier sliced through the dream, jolting her awake. Her heart pounded in her chest as she sat up, the sound still echoing in her ears.

She moved to the window, peering into the darkness. The forest stood still. A palpable sense of being watched lingered.

Gripping her pendant, taking a deep breath. "Whatever secrets you're hiding, I'll find them."

As she settled back into bed, determination steadied her nerves. Tomorrow promised new challenges, and she stood ready to face them head-on.

CHAPTER 2: FIRST IMPRESSIONS

Scene 1: Briefing on Assessment Results

Morning light filtered through the large windows of the main briefing room, casting a warm glow over the assembled specialists. The air buzzed with a mix of anticipation and nervous energy. Kara took a seat near the front, her gaze wandering over the holographic displays cycling through various data streams.

Lieutenant Chas S. Mitchell, a stern-looking officer with sharp features and keen eyes, stepped onto the platform. "Attention!" his voice commanded, and the room fell silent. "Let's get straight to it. We've reviewed the assessment results, and I must say, we have some exceptional results this time."

He began scrolling through the results projected above. "You have been measured. Your performances have been logged. And you have been ranked."

Kara felt a flutter of nerves in her stomach.

Mitchell's gaze swept the room and said, "At the top of the list, and with a new all-time high ranking..."

A murmur rippled through the room. Soldiers started calling out the names of the guys they thought took the honor. "Scott, Khari, Zak. 100 sats on Jojo..."

Lieutenant Mitchell looked dead into Kara's eyes. "Kara Vallian is our new board leader—by far!"

Kara's cheeks warmed as she felt the weight of dozens of eyes turn toward her—some filled with admiration, others with shock and envy.

"Well done, Vallian!" Mitchell said with enthusiasm. "Way to set the bar!"

"Thank you, sir!" keeping her voice steady.

Two disturbing specialists caught her attention. A woman with thick straight black hair and a man with a permanent scowl exchanged glances, their expressions a mix of scorn and hostility.

As Mitchell moved on to other announcements, Kara couldn't shake the unease swirling inside her because of the uncomfortable attention. In a place like this, standing out might not be the safest option.

Scene 2: Subtle Hostility

The hallway outside the briefing room buzzed with loud conversation over Kara's results as personnel filed out. Kara maneuvered through the crowd, hoping to find a quiet space to collect her thoughts.

Kara found herself face to face with the woman she'd noticed earlier. The name tag on her uniform read "Bettz."

"Enjoying the spotlight, superstar?" Bettz sneered, her voice dripping with disdain.

Kara took a deep breath, forcing herself to remain calm. "I'm here to do my job."

The man—Smith, according to his tag—stepped up beside Bettz. "Let's hope you can live up to those scores in the field," his tone making it clear he doubted she could.

Smith scoffed. "Funny how some people get all the luck."

"Luck had nothing to do with it," Kara replied.

Bettz took a step closer. "Careful, new girl. High scores don't make you invincible."

Kara clinched her fist, stepped closer to Bettz, and just then she felt a supportive hand from behind on her shoulder.

"Is there a problem I can help with?" Marcus's friendly voice cut through the tension.

Bettz and Smith exchanged a look before stepping back. "No problem at all," Bettz said with false sweetness. "Just giving a warm welcome to our new superstar."

As they walked away, Marcus said out loud. "Ignore them. They're all bark. Some people can't handle being dominated."

"Thanks," Kara chuckled.

Marcus's eyes lit up. "Let's see some tech!"

Scene 3: Advanced Tech Lab

They made their way to the advanced tech lab. The doors slid open with a soft hiss, revealing a vast space humming with energy and experiments that seemed to defy the laws of physics.

Soft whirs of machinery filled the air, mingling with the glow of holographic interfaces and complex equations scrolling across transparent screens. In one corner, a scientist manipulated what looked like pure energy between her gloved palms in a controlled chamber.

"Impressive, isn't it? I figured you would like a closer look based on your reaction yesterday." Marcus said, watching her take it all in.

Kara's eyes widened as she spotted an array of exoskeleton suits lined up against a wall. "Incredible," she breathed. "I've never seen tech like this."

A woman in a pristine lab coat with dark hair pulled back in a sleek ponytail approached them, her eyes sharp and intelligent behind rimless glasses. "Welcome to the ATL, the Advanced Tech Lab." She extended a hand to Kara. "Dr. Elena Vasquez, head of technological advancements."

Kara shook her hand. "Shukára Vallian, pleasure to meet you."

Dr. Vasquez led them to a sleek, metallic suit standing in a clear case. "This is our latest breakthrough—the XO-1 exoskeleton suit. Each unit enhances physical and mental capabilities beyond human limits."

Kara stared at the suit in awe, her mind racing with the possibilities. "How does it work?" she asked, unable to contain her curiosity.

Dr. Vasquez's eyes lit up at the question. "Interesting. Specialists don't ask about 'how.' Well, it's a fusion of advanced materials science and neural interface technology. The suit doesn't just amplify your strength—it anticipates your movements, enhances your reflexes, it can even accelerate your thought processes."

"I've seen your assessment scores, Shukára," Dr. Vasquez said, a hint of intrigue in her eyes. "We could use someone with your capabilities."

Kara glanced at Marcus's approving nod. "I'd love to contribute in any way I can."

Dr. Vasquez gestured toward the exoskeleton suits. "Care to take one for a test run?"

Kara felt a thrill of excitement. "Absolutely!"

Scene 4: Exoskeleton Suit Test

The simulation arena stretched vast, its boundaries blurred by holographic technology, creating the illusion of endless space. Kara stood in the center, the XO-1 suit conforming to her body like a second skin.

"How does it feel?" Dr. Vasquez's voice came through the communicator.

"Like an extension of myself," flexing her fingers and feeling the suit respond.

"Excellent, let's begin. Remember," Dr. Vasquez continued, "the suit will respond to your thoughts as much as your movements. Trust your instincts."

As the simulation began, Kara felt a surge of energy unlike anything she'd experienced before. The suit moved with her, amplifying her speed and strength to superhuman levels. Holographic opponents appeared and landscapes changed, each more challenging than the last.

Kara moved with a fluid and forceful grace, the suit amplifying her strength and speed. She leaped over barriers, executed precise strikes with superhuman speed, and adapted to the changing environment.

Exhilaration flooded her senses, almost intoxicating. For a moment, she forgot everything else—her mission, her brother, the complexities of covert FOB Epsilon. Only the pure flow of action and reaction remained.

From the observation deck, a small crowd had gathered, pointing in awe, some outright cheering and clapping in amazement. Among them, Zayn watched intently, his stoic expression betraying a hint of admiration. Beside him, Lieutenant Morgan, Captain Reed's assistant, made notes on a tablet with keen interest.

As the simulation concluded, Kara removed her helmet, her face flushed with exhilaration. "That was incredible!" she shouted.

Onlookers could not hold back. They clapped and cheered.

"Your performance, again, exceeded our projections," Dr. Vasquez smiled, expecting an explanation.

Marcus gave her a thumbs-up from behind his post, the control panel. "Told you she was a natural!"

Kara glanced up at the observation deck, glimpsing an approving Zayn before he turned away. Yet, a curious tension hung in the air.

Scene 5: Post-Test Interrogation

After changing out of the suit, adrenaline still pumping, an assistant escorted Kara to a debriefing room. Screens lined the walls, displaying her performance data in intricate detail—reaction times, force outputs, neural patterns. Again, Kara had scored orders of magnitude above the norm.

Captain Reed and Dr. Vasquez entered, their expressions unreadable, with a hint of suppressed excitement.

"Take a seat, Ms. Vallian," Reed motioned to the chair across from them.

Kara sat, her posture composed. "Is there a problem?"

"Not at all," Reed replied in a forced, smooth tone. "In fact, we're quite impressed with your abilities. Your compatibility with the XO-1 is unprecedented...almost."

Dr. Vasquez leaned forward. "We'd like to know more about your background. Any specialized training prior to joining us? Any prior neural synchronizations?"

Kara met their gazes. "Just standard military training. I always push myself to excel. And I never stop. The XO-1, it just felt natural."

"Any family history we should be aware of?" Reed's eyes flicking to the pendant around Kara's neck.

"My parents were both in the service. My brother is..." Kara hesitated. "He was contracting overseas."

Reed arched an eyebrow. "Was?"

Kara held her gaze. "He's missing."

"I see, so sorry to hear," Reed offered, with a hint of something unreadable in her tone. "Well, your skills are exceptional. We believe you could be a valuable asset to some of our specialized projects."

"Such as?" Kara inquired.

"All in due time," Reed half smiled. "For now, continue with your standing assignments."

As they stood to leave, Kara overheard Reed say to Vasquez, "She could be the key."

A chill ran down her spine. What did they mean by that? And why were they interested in my family?

Scene 6: Cafeteria Tensions

Later, Kara entered the bustling cafeteria, the aroma of food mingling with the hum of conversation. She grabbed a tray and scanned the room for a place to sit.

Whispers followed her as she walked. She caught snippets—"That's her," "Top of the class," "Thinks she's all that."

She settled at an empty table, focusing on her meal. A shadow fell over her, and she looked up to see Bettz and Smith standing nearby.

"Mind if we join the prodigy?" Bettz asked with a fake smile.

Kara met her gaze. "Free country."

"Yeah, not really," Bettz replied.

They sat across from her, exchanging smirks. "So, enjoying the VIP treatment?" Smith sneered.

"Really? Still?" Kara losing patience.

"You've been lucky so far in these tests. I think you would crack under real pressure," Bettz's tone dripping with sarcasm.

Kara looked her in the eyes. "A wise woman once told me that luck is when preparation meets opportunity."

"Booooooooooom!" Smith hyped. "I think she just smoked you, Bettz!"

Before Bettz could react, Marcus appeared, setting his tray down beside Kara. "Hey, Kara, got that data you asked for."

Bettz rolled her eyes. "Well, look at that—the golden girl and her sidekick."

"Jealousy doesn't suit you, Bettz." Marcus took a bite of his sandwich.

Smith scoffed. "Watch your back, Vallian. Not everyone around here is as friendly as us."

They stood and walked away, leaving an uncomfortable silence.

Kara sighed. "Thanks for the backup."

Marcus fist bumped Kara. "Anytime, they're just trying to rattle you."

"Well, it's working," she admitted. "What's their beef?"

He gave her a heartfelt look. "Greatness attracts opposition. Don't let them be a distraction."

With a look of fierce intensity, Kara looked at Marcus. "Not a chance!"

Scene 7: Confiding in Marcus

After dinner, Marcus led Kara to an observation deck overlooking the training grounds. The late afternoon sun cast long shadows across the facility, giving everything a surreal, almost otherworldly quality.

"You seemed like you could use a breather." Marcus leaned against the railing.

Kara gazed out at the activity below. "Is it always like this?"

He glanced at her. "The rivalry? Pretty much. Epsilon breeds competition. But there's more to it."

She turned to face him. "What do you mean?"

He hesitated. "Things don't always add up—discrepancies, unusual protocols, experiments that go too far, unanswered questions."

Kara considered his words. "Marcus, I came here looking for answers," she signed. "My brother, Quin—he went missing under strange circumstances. I think this place might be connected."

Marcus's eyes widened. "That's... heavy."

"I know it's a lot to take in," she said.

Marcus's curiosity heightened. "I never heard the name Quin or Vallian around here before you came."

Kara explained, "That's likely because he was an engineering contractor."

Marcus leaned in. "If he was here, he worked in the lower levels of the Advanced Tech Lab. People come and go from the ATL without explanation."

Kara leaned in as well. "I can't shake the feeling that something is off here."

He looked out over the darkening landscape. "Whatever's going on here, it's big. And it's dangerous."

He turned to look Kara in the eyes. "We need to be careful, Kara. I've been digging around myself looking for answers and when you're digging around here, you need to be careful you aren't digging your own grave."

She looked at him with renewed interest. "We can help each other."

He smiled. "I was hoping you'd say that."

Kara nodded, feeling a mix of relief and renewed determination. Not being alone in her suspicions gave her hope. Together, maybe they could uncover the truth—about FOB Epsilon, about Project Chimera, and about what happened to Quin.

Scene 8: Subtle Interactions with Zayn in Training Yard

Over the next few days, Kara immersed herself in training sessions and covert information gathering, pushing her physical and mental limits. She often crossed paths with Zayn, his presence both enigmatic and alluring. Their interactions remained limited to the occasional nod of acknowledgment.

During a grueling combat drill, Kara noticed Zayn observing from the sidelines. His intense gaze followed her movements, and she felt a flutter in her stomach that had nothing to do with exertion.

After the session, as Kara toweled off, she felt a gentle touch on her arm. Zayn had come over, his proximity sending a jolt through her.

"Your form is strong," he remarked.

"Thanks," she replied, catching her breath. "Still room for improvement."

He nodded. "Mind if I offer a suggestion?"

"Please."

He stepped closer and lowered her stance with a gentle touch. "Keep your center of gravity lower. It'll give you more stability," his breath warm against her ear.

He had adjusted her position lower, his firm hands gentle to the touch.

She looked up at him, their faces mere inches apart. "Like this?"

"Perfect," his eyes meeting hers. A moment of charged silence hung between them before he stepped back. "You're a quick learner."

"Good teacher," offering a faint smile.

He gave a slight nod. "Keep it up. You have the touch."

As he walked away, Kara couldn't help but feel the growing connection.

Kara's heart raced, and not just from the exercise. Something about Zayn captured her—a connection she couldn't deny. As he walked away, she noticed Marcus watching them, an insightful smile playing on his face.

Marcus gave her an upward head nod and an eyebrow raise, looking at Zayn followed by a big smile looking at her. Kara huffed, shook her head, and turned her back on him and his "humor."

Marcus laughed and carried on. That had made his day!

Scene 9: Late-Night Data Center Spy Work

Later that night, driven by a shared sense of purpose, Kara and Marcus dug deeper into the base's secrets. Under the cover of darkness, they made their way to the restricted data center.

The corridors sat quiet. Kara's heart pounded in her chest, every shadow seeming to hide a potential threat.

"Are you sure you can do this?" she whispered as they reached the secured entrance.

Marcus nodded. "If we're going to find out what happened to Quin, this is our best shot. Just keep watch while I work my magic."

Marcus tapped on the keypad with practiced ease. "I've disabled the cameras. We have a small window."

They slipped inside, the glow of monitors casting eerie shadows. Marcus began hacking into the system while Kara kept watch.

She kept her eyes on the corridor, every nerve on high alert. The minutes ticked by.

Marcus let out a soft exclamation of triumph. "I'm in," he said, his fingers flying over the holographic interface. "Let's see what secrets you're hiding, Project Chimera."

Kara leaned in, her eyes widening as classified files appeared. In them, references to inter-dimensional travel, to beings with extraordinary abilities, to experiments that defied the laws of physics as she understood them!

And there, buried in a subfolder, a file with Quin's name!

Just as Kara reached out to open it, a piercing alarm shattered the silence. Red lights flashed, and the sound of running footsteps echoed in the distance.

"Security breach detected," an automated voice announced.

"We're compromised!" Marcus exclaimed.

"Can you shut it down?" Kara asked.

"No time. We need to get out of here!"

Footsteps echoed in the corridor outside. Kara scanned the room. "There must be another way!" A door at the back caught her eye. "This way!"

They darted out the back just as the main doors burst open with security personnel.

Scene 10: A Moment of Connection

As they raced through the maze-like corridors, alarms blaring around them, Kara and Marcus found themselves at a dead end with their detection and arrest imminent! Kara prepared to fight. And just as despair set in, a panel in the wall slid open, revealing a hidden passageway illuminated by emergency lights.

Zayn stood in the opening, his expression intense, and his voice calm. "Care to join me?" he urged, ushering them inside.

"Zayn!" Kara gasped.

As the panel closed behind them, plunging them into relative quiet, Kara found herself pressed close to Zayn in the narrow passage. His presence radiated both comfort and a thrilling intensity.

For a moment, the world seemed to shrink to just the two of them. Kara felt a connection, a spark of something that both thrilled and perplexed her. "You knew I would be here."

"You shouldn't be here," Zayn's silver-blue eyes searching hers.

"I had to know," her voice barely audible. "About my brother, about what's going on here."

Something flickered in Zayn's eyes—understanding, perhaps even admiration. "We're not so different," his tone softer than she'd ever heard it. "I'm also looking for Quin. I'm also here for a greater purpose."

"How did you know about her brother? How did you know where to find us? Greater purpose?" Marcus catching his breath.

Zayn looked deep into Shukára's eyes. "I'm here to stop Project Chimera. I saw your brother going down the same path you are on. When I saw you in the corridors tonight, I knew you would end up here, running for your life. I couldn't let you get captured, too."

Marcus cleared his throat as Project Chimera security searched on the other side of the wall. "Not to interrupt," he said, "but can we keep moving?"

Zayn nodded. "I'll lead you to safety. But be cautious. The walls have ears."

As they made their way through the hidden passage, Kara's mind raced. Zayn knows more than he lets on. Could she trust him? And Project Chimera is about "beings with 'abilities'" and "inter-dimensional travel?" Does Marcus have secrets too? How well did Zayn know Quin? What else is Zayn hiding?

They followed Zayn through a series of twists and turns until they emerged outside near the forest's edge.

Kara grabbed Zayn by the arm. "Explain! What do you know about Quin?"

Zayn put his hand on hers. "You are stirring forces that are dangerous and that you don't understand."

She stepped closer. "Then help me understand!"

Scene 11: An Unsettling Observer

Their conversation cut short. In the shadows stood Lieutenant Morgan. Morgan had a blank expression as they watched Kara, Zayn and Marcus. The lieutenant made no move to approach or raise an alarm.

A chill ran down Kara's spine. Morgan—ally or adversary? Friend or foe? The lieutenant's silent observation added yet another layer of mystery to the already complex web surrounding the covert FOB Epsilon.

As they set to part ways, each to head back to their individual quarters to avoid suspicion, Kara couldn't shake the feeling that they had just crossed a point of no return. The walls seemed to close in, the secrets of Forward Operating Base Epsilon looming larger than ever.

"Be careful, Kara," Zayn whispered before leaving in the opposite direction.

She watched him go, her mind a whirlwind of questions.

Thinking back to the file bearing Quin's name, the mention of beings and new laws of physics, the connection she'd felt with Zayn, and the silent presence of Lieutenant Morgan, Kara understood a few things for certain: the stakes had never been higher, her involvement ran deeper than ever, and she had drawn closer to the truth than ever before. No matter the price, she would see this through to the end.

CHAPTER 3: WHISPERS OF THE UNKNOWN

Scene 1: Unsettling Hearsay

The mess hall buzzed with nervous energy, a stark contrast to its usual military precision. Kara sat with Marcus, eager to discuss the revelations of last night, and to make sense of it, eager to find Zayn and get answers.

Fragments of hushed conversations grew louder and drifted around them like leaves in an autumn wind.

"Did you hear?" a soldier whispered two tables over. "Animals torn apart, nothing eaten. No predator tracks. Sounds like they are trying to spook us."

"The lights in the forest..." another voice carried. "Green and violet, just like The Storm."

The soldier fell silent as Captain Reed strode past, her boots clicking against the polished floor with measured precision.

Kara's hand moved to her pendant. The same colors as the storm during her arrival. The same ethereal hues that had filled the sky the night she and Quin received their pendants all those many years ago. Her fork clattered against her plate.

"You okay?" Marcus moved closer, his voice low and concerned.

"Those lights they mentioned," Kara leaned in, "they sound like—"

"The storm during our landings," Marcus finished. "I know. And no storms like that have ever been recorded in this region."

A commotion outside near the entrance drew their attention. A local farmer, his weathered face pale with fear, gestured as he told a story of something terrifying he had seen.

The gate patrol soldier ushered him away, but his emotions hung in the air like a heavy fog. Kara felt her pulse quicken. Something about his gesturing and expression tugged at a memory. It seemed somehow related to their recent discoveries.

"Marcus," she whispered, "I need access to those Project Chimera files. These incidents, Quin's disappearance—they're connected. I can feel it."

Marcus glanced around. "The files will be more heavily encrypted and secured now. But... I might have another way in. Just need time to—"

The intercom crackled to life: "All personnel report to main briefing room at 0900 hours. Attendance is mandatory."

Kara met Marcus's eyes. The same understanding passed between them—whatever unfolded in the forest and on the base had grown too big to ignore.

As they made their way to the briefing room, Kara caught glimpses of nervous faces and heard whispered theories. But beneath the fear and speculation, she sensed something else—a current of energy that seemed to pulse through the walls of the base, like a heartbeat growing stronger.

The pendant felt warm against her skin, and for a moment, she could have sworn it hummed in harmony with that unseen pulse.

Scene 2: Briefing on Mysterious Disturbances

The main briefing room thrummed with activity, the air thick with tension and the indistinct murmur of voices. Holographic displays flickered with images of mutilated livestock, strange energy readings, and thermal scans of the surrounding forest, revealing illogical heat signatures moving against the wind.

Captain Reed stood at the podium, her usual commanding presence somehow heightened. The room fell silent as she activated a larger hologram showing a map of the region, red markers indicating incident locations.

"Over the past week," her voice cutting through the silence, "we've recorded twenty-one unusual occurrences around the base. The local peoples are overwhelmed, and their unrest is growing."

The map zoomed in on the most recent incidents. Kara noticed they formed an almost perfect circle around the base.

"We're launching an investigation," Reed continued. "We need volunteers for reconnaissance tea—"

"I volunteer," Kara standing before she could stop herself. The pendant seemed to pulse against her skin, urging her forward.

Across the room, she saw Zayn rise as well, his silver-blue eyes meeting hers with an intensity that made her breath catch. "I volunteer as well," his deep voice carrying through the quiet room.

Captain Reed's lips curved in what might have been a smile—or a smirk. "Specialist Vallian, Agent Zayn. How... fortuitous." She made a note on her tablet. "Report to Equipment Bay 3 at 1100 hours. Full tactical gear."

As the briefing continued, Kara felt the weight of unseen eyes upon her. She turned to find Lieutenant Morgan watching her with an unreadable expression. Their face betrayed nothing, but Kara couldn't shake the feeling that they had expected her to volunteer, perhaps somehow even orchestrated it.

Around her, other teams assembled, but her focus remained on the map. The incident locations, when connected, didn't just form a circle—they seemed to form a pattern similar to the one etched into her pendant.

She glanced at Zayn and found him already watching her, his hand resting on something beneath his uniform collar. Their eyes locked, and in that instant, Kara knew for sure—they were both caught up in something that went far beyond military protocol or standard operations.

The pendant warmed again, and this time she felt certain she heard it—a faint, crystalline hum hinting at something deeper, whispering of ancient secrets and destined paths.

Scene 3: Journey to the Village

The armored hovercraft cut through the morning mist, its quiet hum a stark contrast to the primordial silence of the surrounding forest. Zayn piloted with practiced ease, his movements fluid and precise. Kara sat beside him, watching the ancient trees slide past like silent sentinels.

Aware of Zayn's hesitance to discuss Quin, she measured her approach. "Can we talk about Quin and about what we saw in the files?"

Zayn continued to pilot for a moment, as if determining how much to disclose or where to start. "The villagers call this the Whispering Wood," breaking the silence. His voice carried an undertone of something Kara couldn't quite place—knowledge, perhaps, or warning. "They say it remembers."

"Remembers what? Remembers Quin?" Kara asked, noticing how the mist seemed to curl away from their vehicle rather than the vehicle disturbing it.

A shadow of concern crossed his face. "Everything."

The forest grew denser, older. Gnarled branches reached across their path like grasping fingers, forcing Zayn to navigate with increasing care. Kara's pendant grew warmer with each passing mile, its heat matching the strange tension building in her chest.

"You feel it too, don't you?" Zayn whispered.

Before she could answer, a massive wolf appeared in their path, its fur shimmering in an ethereal silver shade. Their eyes met through the windshield, and Kara gasped—its eyes held the same otherworldly blue as Zayn's. For a heartbeat, time seemed to stop.

Then the wolf turned and vanished into the mist, leaving no tracks in the damp earth.

"Did you—" Kara started.

"Yes." Zayn's knuckles turning white on the controls. "We're close now."

The village emerged from the mist like a painting coming into focus. Ancient stone buildings stood in harmony with the forest, their walls covered in vines that seemed to pulse with a faint, luminescent glow. Smoke rose from chimneys in spiral patterns that defied the wind.

As they parked the hovercraft, Kara noticed the villagers emerging from their homes. Their faces held neither fear nor surprise—only solemn expectation.

Scene 4: Meeting Elder Tomas

The villagers moved aside, creating a path toward the largest structure—a circular building where stone and living wood intertwined, as if the forest had grown into these walls rather than human hands building them. At its entrance stood Elder Tomas, his presence commanding despite his advanced age.

Time had carved deep lines into his face, but his eyes blazed with an inner fire that made Kara's pendant pulse in response. He wore robes of deep blue, embroidered with symbols that matched those on her pendant with uncanny precision.

"The forest told us you were coming," his voice resonating with the strength of ancient oak. "When the veil grows thin, the Guardians must answer."

Kara felt Zayn stiffen beside her. The elder's gaze moved between them, settling on her pendant.

"Come," he gestured toward the building's entrance. "There are truths that must be spoken before darkness falls."

Inside, crystals illuminated the circular chamber, casting ever-shifting patterns of light across walls adorned with intricate murals. Kara's military training cataloged exits and defensive positions, yet her attention gravitated toward the center of the room, where a pool of water reflected inexplicable depths.

Elder Tomas stood before the pool, his shadow stretching and moving in the crystal light. When he spoke again, his voice carried the weight of centuries.

"In times of old, when the worlds were young and the boundaries between realms stood firm, there were those chosen to maintain the balance." His eyes fixed on Kara's pendant. "They wore the marks of their calling, passed down through blood and destiny."

He moved to a mural showing figures holding familiar-looking pendants, standing against a tide of darkness. "But pride and fear grew in the hearts of men. They sought to control what was meant to remain free, to bind what must flow like water between worlds."

His voice took on a rhythmic quality that seemed to resonate with the surrounding stones: "Our children's rhyme tells the tale. 'When shadow seeks to bind the light, and fear would cage the wildest night, the ancient blood must rise once more, to guard what was and what is in store.'"

The pool's surface rippled without a touch. "Your brother understood this truth, Shukára Vallian. He saw what your military seeks to control, what they cannot comprehend. The question that remains..." his eyes seemed to pierce through her, "is whether you are ready to see it, too."

Kara's hand clutched her pendant, which now burned against her skin. "What happened to Quin?" she demanded, her voice steady despite the trembling in her soul.

Elder Tomas raised his hand, and the crystals' light dimmed. "I see him beyond the Realmbridge—touched by veilrot but not yet Shadowbound. The same force that brought you here creates the energy that even now gathers in the forest. The veil between worlds thins, young one. And with it comes both danger and destiny."

Zayn moved closer to Kara, his presence reassuring yet charged with unspoken tension. The elder's eyes moved to him, a knowing look crossing his weathered features.

"The wolf marks its chosen well," he said. "But even ancient Guardians must bow before the storm that comes, even if they too are the storm."

Scene 5: Confrontation in the Forest

Dusk approached as Kara and Zayn exited the circular structure of stone and living wood.

Ancient warnings from the elder echoed in their minds.

During their meeting, the forest had transformed—or perhaps they truly saw it for the first time. The path back to their armored transport stretched longer, the pathways empty of the townsfolk who had guided them to the elder. Around them, trees whispered with ancient voices, their branches swaying in a nonexistent wind.

"Realmbridges! Veilrot! Shadowbound! Is he crazy or am I crazy for almost believing him back there? We need to get back. I'll radio base." Kara reached for her comm unit. Static crackled through the speaker, punctuated by sounds that might have been words in a transcendental language.

"Technology fails when the veil thins," Zayn murmured, his hand drifting to what Kara now realized as his own pendant, previously hidden beneath his uniform. "We're on our own."

The mist thickened around them, forming shapes that vanished when looked at. Their boots made no sound on the damp earth, as if the forest held its breath.

A distant howl shattered the silence—the same haunting call Kara had heard from her quarters. But this time, another sound answered it, a wrong sound.

"Zayn—" she started, but he stepped forward, positioning himself between her and the shadows in the trees.

They emerged like ink bleeding through paper—shapes that defied natural law, their forms shifting between beast and shadow. Eyes that gleamed with a yellow light fixed upon them. Kara's military training screamed at her to fire, to fight, to run—but her pendant pulsed with a different warning.

She raised her rifle anyway, squeezing off three precise shots. The bullets passed through the creatures like smoke, leaving swirling patterns in their wake.

"Conventional weapons won't work." Tension laced Zayn's voice. "Kara, whatever you see next... trust that I'm still me."

Before she could question his words, the nearest shadowy creature lunged. Zayn moved with superhuman speed, his eyes beginning to glow with the same silver-blue light she'd seen in the wolf. Energy crackled around him like contained lightning, and when he struck at the creature, his hand left luminescent trails in the air.

The shadow-creature recoiled with a screech that seemed to come from everywhere and nowhere. Its companions circled, their forms rippling with malevolent purpose.

"The pendant," Zayn called out between strikes, his movements a dance of light against dark. "It's not just a symbol, Kara. It's like a key. Your brother knew—he learned to call upon his. You can too!"

Against her skin, the pendant burned, its heat spreading through her chest. Reality shifted, peeling back like layers of an onion to reveal currents of energy she'd never seen before. Dark tears appeared in the fabric of existence where the shadow-creatures leaked evil into their world.

A surge—familiar yet alien—coursed through her. Her hand moved to the pendant of its own accord, and light exploded outward, forcing the creatures back. For a moment, she saw everything with painful clarity—the layers of reality, the thinning barriers between worlds, and Zayn's true nature blazing like a wolf made of light in human form.

"Impossible," she whispered, but the word felt hollow. She'd seen too much now to disbelieve impossible things.

The shadow-creatures retreated, their forms dissipating like smoke in strong wind, leaving behind an unnatural silence. Kara stared at her hands, still feeling the jolt that had coursed through her.

"What... what was that?" her voice shook.

Zayn turned to her, the glow fading from his eyes but not disappearing. "That... was your birthright awakening."

Scene 6: Zayn's Revelation

They found a small clearing, the events of the past hour hanging between them like an unspoken weight. Moonlight filtered through the canopy, casting dappled shadows that seemed to dance with newfound significance.

Zayn sat on a fallen log, his composure perfect despite what had just transpired. "I'm a Guardian," breaking the tense silence. "One of those chosen to maintain the balance between realms. Just as you are meant to be."

Kara remained standing, her mind racing to process everything. "Twin Guardians will be born... and the wolf we saw earlier?"

"A manifestation of my true nature," he nodded. "Each Guardian resonates with different aspects of the natural and supernatural world. The wolf chose me, just as other forces will align with you."

"And Quin?" Her voice cracking on her brother's name. "He knew about all this?"

"He discovered the truth during his work here. Project Chimera isn't just a military research initiative, Kara. They're trying to control forces they don't understand, to weaponize the barriers between worlds. The veilrot of which the elder speaks; Project

Chimera creates it. It is corruption deep enough to create realmscars or tears in reality. And worse, I fear Project Chimera has Quin imprisoned." Zayn's eyes flickered with that otherworldly light again. "Your brother tried to stop them. That's why—"

"That's why he disappeared," Kara finished, her hand tightening around her pendant. "Where is he? Why didn't he tell me? We shared everything."

Zayn stood, moving closer to her. "I don't know where he is. He was protecting you. But he also left you clues—the pendant, the patterns, the path that led you here. He knew you'd understand when the time was right."

The pendant pulsed, as if confirming his words. Kara looked up at Zayn, seeing him now—the ancient thunder contained within human form, the weight of responsibility in his eyes.

"Show me," she whispered. "Show me everything."

Scene 7: Growing Intimacy

Everything felt different—as if the world had shifted on its axis. Or perhaps Kara had changed, her awareness expanding to encompass layers of reality she'd never known existed. The mist that curled around them now carried whispers of ancient secrets, and even the darkness between the trees seemed alive with possibility.

Zayn, now at her side, his presence both comforting and electrifying. When their hands brushed, a spark of energy passed between them, causing the nearby leaves to stir without wind.

"Sorry," he murmured, but didn't move away. "Our energies are... resonating."

Kara studied his profile in the moonlight, seeing both the man and something more. "How do you handle it?" she asked. "Knowing what you are, what's out there, while pretending to be..."

"Normal?" A slight smile touched his lips. "The same way you've handled carrying that pendant all these years. Some part of you always knew it was more than just jewelry."

She touched the pendant. "The night we received these... the old woman... I always thought of her as some local mystic that my parents tolerated out of politeness. But she knew, didn't she? About all of this?"

Zayn nodded, his hands embracing her arms. "The Guardians have always found ways to preserve their legacy, to prepare the next generation. Even if that preparation had to be subtle."

The air seemed to crackle with an unspoken connection. Shukára felt drawn to him on some deeper, primal level—as if their essences recognized each other.

"We should focus," she said, breaking the moment. "Project Chimera, Quin, these shadow-creatures—"

"Shadowrends," Zayn interrupted, "they tear through reality when the veil thins."

Kara absorbed the new reality. "There's so much at stake."

"Yes," he agreed. His hand found hers in the darkness, fingers intertwining. "But we're stronger together. That's why the ancients are awakening now—they know what's coming."

Scene 8: Debrief with Captain Reed

Captain Reed's office felt suffocatingly normal after everything they'd witnessed. The sterile military efficiency, the harsh fluorescent lighting—it all seemed like a thin veneer over a much deeper reality.

"Report," Reed commanded from behind her desk, her eyes sharp as she studied them.

Kara and Zayn exchanged a brief glance, a silent agreement to reveal only what was necessary.

"The village elder shared local legends about the forest," Kara began. "They believe the disturbances are connected to old traditions about boundaries weakening between worlds."

"Superstitious nonsense," Reed dismissed, but something in her tone rang false. "And the attacked livestock?"

"No signs of conventional predators," Zayn replied. "The villagers are frightened but managing. Elder Tomas seems to have them well organized."

Reed's fingers drummed on her desk—the only sign of her inner tension. "This Elder Tomas... did he mention anything about artifacts? Ancient symbols, perhaps?"

Kara felt her pendant burn against her skin, as if warning her. "Only vague references to local mythology," she lied, keeping her voice steady.

"I see." Reed's gaze lingered on them both, calculating. "Write up your full reports by morning. Dismissed."

As they turned to leave, Reed spoke again. "Oh, and Specialist Vallian? That's an interesting pendant you wear. Family heirloom?"

"Yes, ma'am," Kara replied without turning back. "Just a keepsake."

The door closed behind them with a final click.

Scene 9: Chance Encounter with Morgan

The corridor outside Reed's office seemed longer than usual, the shadows deeper. Lieutenant Morgan emerged, stepping out from a side passage.

Their eyes met as they passed. Morgan's expression unreadable, but Kara felt a subtle shift in the air—like the calm before a storm.

They exchanged no words, but the weight of Morgan's gaze followed them down the hallway. Zayn's hand brushed Kara's back, ushering her around the corner.

"Morgan knows something," Kara whispered.

"Morgan knows many things," Zayn responded. "The question is, whose side are they on?"

Scene 10: A Silent Warning Note

Exhaustion weighed on Kara as she entered her quarters, the events of the day swirling in her mind like winds in a storm. The room felt different now—the shadows held new meaning, the air seemed charged with potential. Her enhanced awareness picked up subtle energies she'd never noticed before, making the familiar space feel almost alien.

She moved to the window, drawn by an inexplicable urge to check the forest. The moonlight painted the trees in silvery hues, and for a moment, she thought she saw that mysterious wolf again, its ethereal form ghosting between the trunks. A sentinel—Zayn's other self—watching over them all.

As she turned from the window, something caught her eye—a slip of paper on her pillow that hadn't been there before. Her military training kicked in as she approached it, scanning for signs of entry. The door locks... check, the window seals... unbroken, yet...

The note lay there, written in an elegant, flowing script that seemed to shimmer in the moonlight:

"Be careful who you trust. Not all who wear masks know they wear them."

The paper felt strange under her fingers, almost alive, and she noticed that the ink shifted color as she tilted it—from deep black to a familiar violet-green, the same colors as the storm that had brought her here.

A deep howl pierced the night—closer than ever before. The sound resonated with her pendant, sending vibrations through her chest that felt like words just beyond comprehension. But this time, instead of fear, she felt recognition. The howl cried out, not of danger, but a call to action, to destiny.

Kara moved to her nightstand, where the photo of her and Quin still stood. The elderly woman who had given them their pendants seemed to stare out from the image with new significance. In the background, those strange lights she'd always dismissed as film artifacts now pulsed with obvious power.

"I understand now," she whispered to Quin's smiling image, "why you couldn't tell me everything... why you had to let me find my own way here."

She tucked the mysterious note into her journal, alongside her sketches of the village elder's murals and the symbols that matched her pendant.

Project Chimera, shadowrends bleeding through thinning veil between worlds—all connected. And somewhere in the center of it all, Quin left breadcrumbs for her to follow.

Another howl echoed through the night, met by distant sounds defying natural law.

The war between worlds escalated, and now she was part of it.

She touched her pendant, sensing a dormant force stirring to life within it, and within herself.

Through the window, the forest seemed to pulse with ethereal energy. Tomorrow promised new opportunities, new challenges, new revelations. For now, she allowed herself a moment to absorb the truth of who and what she had begun to become.

A flash of violet-green lightning illuminated the trees in the distance, and for just a moment, Kara thought she saw the shapes seen earlier in the village forest, now moving against the sky—ancient forces arising as the veil grew thinner.

What clues do Project Chimera's files reveal about Quin and Captain Reed's reckless plans? She whispered into the night, her voice carrying the weight of newfound purpose: "I'm coming, Quin. And this time, I understand what we're fighting for."

The pendant warmed against her skin in response, harmonizing with the eternal song of the realms—a melody she began to hear.

CHAPTER 4: THE VEIL UNRAVELED

Scene 1: Breaking Into the Restricted Archives

The base's central data core hummed with artificial life, its servers casting a blue glow through the darkened facility. Kara moved through the shadows, her enhanced awareness making her hyperconscious of every energy signature—the electric pulse of security systems, the subtle vibrations of cooling fans, and something else, something deeper that felt like a wound in reality.

"The maintenance window starts in three minutes," Marcus whispered through their encrypted comms. "You'll have seventeen minutes before the systems recycle."

Beside her, Zayn moved with predatory grace, his presence both reassuring and dangerous. Since the forest encounter, Kara found herself aware of the caged storm contained within him. His eyes flickered in the darkness, catching hints of that otherworldly blue when the security cameras turned away.

"There's something wrong here," Kara murmured, her pendant growing warm against her skin. "The energy... it's twisted."

Zayn nodded. "Project Chimera's experiments leave scars in the fabric of reality. You're sensing the damage they've done to the natural barriers between worlds."

Marcus's voice crackled through their earpieces: "Okay, the security loop is engaging... now. You're clear to move."

They approached the main archive door, its reinforced steel frame humming with both electronic and—Kara now realized—supernatural countermeasures. As Marcus began his remote hack, Kara placed her hand near the door's surface, not quite touching it. The pendant pulsed, revealing layers of sickly green energy writhing beneath the mundane security systems.

"They've warded it," Zayn said. "But we can break through." He looked at Kara with concerning eyes. "They've gotten further along than I expected."

Kara understood. The shadowrends had been impervious to bullets, yet vulnerable to them and their pendants. Likewise, these barriers held weaknesses they, the Guardians, could exploit. She closed her eyes, remembering how the energy had flowed through her in the forest. Warmth spread from the pendant, its tendrils of light emanating and extending through the warped barriers.

Marcus's hack clicked the electronic lock open, but the supernatural ward remained—until Kara's awakening abilities pushed against it. Before them, sickly energy shuddered and parted like a curtain.

"I'm in their systems," Marcus reported, his voice tense with concentration. "But there's something odd about the data architecture. It's like... like the information is alive somehow. It's adapting while I'm in it."

"It is alive," Zayn confirmed, scanning the rows of servers with his otherworldly sight. "They're not just storing data—they're trying to capture and contain the supernatural. Supernatural Intelligence was never meant to be controlled or caged in silicon and circuits."

Marcus questioned. "You mean AI? Right?"

Zayn muted the comms. "This is beyond AI."

Kara and Zayn moved deeper into the server farms, where the air grew thick with forbidden energy. Holographic displays flickered with equations and diagrams that twisted in unusual ways when viewed. Kara's instincts screamed that none of this should exist, while her awakened Guardian senses could feel the fundamental wrongness of Project Chimera.

"Look for anything related to interdimensional research," Kara's fingers dancing through holographic images while her pendant guided her through the encrypted files. "Quin would have left traces of his discoveries, something to—"

She stopped. There, buried beneath layers of classified data, a folder marked with a symbol identical to the one on her pendant. And the file name made her heart skip: "Project Chimera: Guardian Protocol."

The holographic files cast a sickly green glow across Kara's face. "Wait," she frowned. "Look at this."

She expanded a personal log entry, dated three years ago. In it, a woman's face appeared—younger, untwisted by corruption, wearing a familiar uniform.

"Doctor Sarah Reed," her voice came through steady but tired. "Project lead. Another breach in Sector 7 today. Three civilians dead before we could contain it. Natural supernatural entities keep bleeding through dimensional walls—no warning, no pattern. The military wants to build bigger walls, set up more gun emplacements. They don't understand that conventional weapons are useless against these incursions."

The log flickered. Reed looked haunted now, dark circles under her eyes. "The entity that killed those people? It was a child once. A little girl who got too close to a dimensional tear... it changed her. We couldn't save her. We couldn't even give her parents a body to bury."

Kara felt her pendant grow cold. "She's talking about saving children."

"Containment protocols failing again," Reed's voice continued. "The old methods aren't working. If we can't control it, study it, regulate it... how many more children will we lose? How many more families torn apart? There has to be a better way."

The log ended. Kara looked at Zayn. "She was trying to help people."

"By trying to control what she doesn't understand. And somewhere along the way," Zayn said, "her mission became corrupted. Just like her methods."

Kara, studying Reed's younger face. "We need to understand them better, not just fight them."

Scene 2: Discovery and Danger

The alarms erupted with both electronic shrieks and something deeper—a subsonic wail that made Kara's teeth ache. Red emergency lights strobed through the archive, but they flickered with unnatural patterns, as if reality protested Project Chimera's violations.

"We've got company!" Marcus's voice crackled through their comms. "Multiple security teams converging on your position, and… wait, what the hell? These readings don't make sense—"

"They're not just sending human forces," Zayn cut in, his voice tight with tension. His eyes blazed that ethereal blue as he scanned through the walls. "They're activating containment protocols—ethereal containment."

The temperature in the room plummeted. Frost crystallized on the servers in patterns that resembled the symbols from Elder Tomas's murals. The pendant burned against Kara's skin, warning of approaching danger from multiple realities.

"Marcus, get out now," Kara commanded, closing the classified files with swift waves of her hand through the holograms. "Wipe any trace of your presence in the system. If they catch you—"

"Already gone," Marcus replied, but she heard the tremor in his voice. "But guys… something's happening to the base's grid. Energy fluctuations like I've never seen. There are—there are terawatts being stored… and fluctuating—fluctuating intentionally in patterns, between the zones."

Zayn grabbed Kara's arm, pulling her away from the terminal. "They're using the base grid to fuel their containment fields. We need to move… now!"

That brief contact sent electricity through her veins. Even in danger, she couldn't ignore how her energy hummed in response to his proximity.

They sprinted toward their planned escape route, but the corridor ahead shimmered with a sickly green barrier of both energy and shadow—the same tainted force Kara had sensed in the door's wards, but far stronger. Behind them, heavy boots thundered on metal flooring, accompanied by an odd chittering inhuman sound.

"Options?" Kara backed into Zayn as they found themselves trapped between approaching threats.

"One," his form shimmered with that contained storm she'd witnessed in the forest. "But you'll have to trust me."

The chittering grew louder. Shadowrends oozed through the walls. They appeared both manufactured and defiled, their yellow eyes tinged with the same sickly green as Project Chimera's barriers.

"Whatever you're going to do," Kara said, her pendant pulsing in sync with Zayn's energy, "do it fast!"

Zayn turned. "Hug me!"

Kara turned around. "What?"

He pulled Kara close. "I'm aligning our pendants."

Zayn's essence exploded outward, his human form transforming into a beacon of silver-blue light. The containment field shuddered as he pressed against it, not with force but with pure, natural energy—the antithesis of Project Chimera's twisted technology. Still, the effort fell short. Sweat beaded on his forehead as the barrier held firm.

"Together," Kara realized. She pulled him closer, reaching deep for that well she'd touched in the forest. The pendants blazed with light as she felt the surge from Zayn flowing into her, and hers into him, intertwining, building.

"Now!" they shouted in unison.

A combined eruption surged outward in an expansive wave. The containment field shattered like green glass, its fragments dissolving into nothing. The manufactured shadow-creatures recoiled, their forms destabilizing as natural law reasserted.

"This way!" Zayn pulled her through the dissolving barrier, their hands locked together, swells still flowing between them. Behind them, human shouts mixed with inhuman shrieks as their escape route sealed itself with pure Guardian energy.

They ran through corridors that blurred between the normal and the supernatural, their enhanced senses guiding them through the chaos. But both of them knew this marked only the beginning. They'd seen too much, learned too much—Project Chimera would never stop hunting them now.

"Marcus," Kara panted into her comm as they ran, "meet us at emergency exit point Charlie. And Marcus... prepare yourself. After tonight, nothing's going to be the same."

Scene 3: The Assistant's Dilemma

Lieutenant Morgan sat alone in the security hub, surrounded by screens showing the chaos unfolding throughout the base. One monitor displayed Captain Reed barking orders as she strode toward the archive, flanked by soldiers carrying weapons that pulsed with unnatural energy. Another showed the manufactured shadowrends slithering through walls, their movements jerky and wrong—a perversion of the natural order.

But Morgan fixated on the center screen, where Kara and Zayn's fusion had shattered the containment field. The display flickered and distorted, unable to capture the pure energy they'd released.

"So it's true," Morgan's fingers hovering over the security controls. "Natural Guardians. Not lab-created like—"

The thought remained unfinished as urgent requests for security authorization flooded the system. Protocols demanded immediate lockdown—sealing all exits, activating every containment measure in Project Chimera's arsenal.

Morgan's hand trembled over the controls.

Images flashed through memory: test subjects screaming as Project Chimera tried to force Guardian essence into unprepared vessels; the sickly green corruption, veilrot, spreading through reality; Captain Reed's bitter smile as she explained it all as "necessary for humanity's protection."

The security system pinged again, demanding action.

Morgan took a deep breath and began manipulating the security hologram panel, fingers flying, tapping multiple controls. Surveillance cameras began showing looped footage. Containment fields flickered and failed at crucial junctions. Security doors opened and closed to create a path to the eastern exit.

"Oops," Morgan's tone mischievous. "System malfunction. How inopportune."

A final command executed, and the hub's main console sparked, sending up a thin tendril of smoke. By the time backup systems came online, the damage would be done.

Morgan stood, straightening an already immaculate uniform, and headed for the door. There would be questions later, investigations. But sometimes choosing a side meant burning bridges you couldn't return to.

In the corridor outside, Captain Reed's voice echoed through the comm system: "Find them! I want them alive. The Guardians must not escape!"

Morgan allowed a small, grim smile. "Too late," the lieutenant whispered, and walked toward the chaos, the perfect picture of a dutiful officer responding to an emergency.

Scene 4: Escape to the Forest

Marcus waited at the emergency exit point, his holographic glasses projecting the security failures across the base that he hadn't caused. His fingers pushed through the images projecting in front of him, trying to make sense of energy readings that defied the laws of physics.

The door burst open. Kara and Zayn emerged at a run, their forms haloed by residual energy that made his holo-glasses crack in spiderweb patterns.

"Don't ask questions," Kara said. "Just run!"

They sprinted toward the tree line as searchlights swept the perimeter. Behind them, inhuman shrieks mixed with the base's alarms in a cacophony of chaos. Marcus glanced back and froze mid-stride.

"Oh my god," he whispered.

Shadowrends oozed through the base's walls like living ink, their yellow eyes leaving trails of sickly light. But something even more disturbing followed—soldiers encased in armor pulsing with unnatural green energy, their movements jerky and puppet-like.

"Keep moving!" Zayn grabbed Marcus's arm, pulling him forward. "The forest will protect us!"

"The forest, will what?" Marcus stumbled as they entered the tree line. His basis of reality crumbling with each step. "Kara, what's happening? What were those things? And is Zayn... glowing?"

"Remember all those system anomalies we couldn't explain?" Kara vaulted over a fallen log, her pendant blazing with light. "They weren't system errors. Project Chimera isn't just a military research division—they're trying to weaponize supernatural forces."

A search drone buzzed overhead, but the forest canopy seemed to shift, branches interweaving to hide them from view. Marcus stared upward, his face pale in the moonlight.

"That's not... trees don't..." he swallowed hard. "This is impossible!"

"Your impossible is our reality," Zayn said, his eyes flaring that ethereal blue. "Look."

He raised his hand, and pure energy coursed from him in a wave that turned aside a group of pursuing shadowrends. They dissolved like smoke in the wind, their shrieks echoing through the trees.

Marcus's knees buckled. Kara caught him before he lost his balance, and he stared at her pendant, pulsing in sync with Zayn. "I don't understand. All this time, when we were searching the files... you knew?"

"Not until recently," Kara helped him steady. "But now you know why we have to stop them. Project Chimera isn't just researching these new found realities—Project Chimera is destroying our core base realities."

A howl echoed through the forest—that same thunderous howl Kara had heard before. But this time, she understood its meaning. "They're coming," she said. "Real supernatural forces, not Project Chimera's corrupted versions. We need to move!"

Marcus took a shaky breath, pulling himself together. "Okay. Okay. I'm processing. Sort of. But..." he pulled out his tablet, now displaying readings he'd never seen before, "if this is real, if all of this is real, then maybe I can help track these energy patterns. Maybe science and... whatever this is... can work together?"

Zayn smiled. "That's what Project Chimera thought. The difference is, you're asking 'how can I understand and help' instead of 'how can I control?'"

Another howl, closer now. The forest seemed to reverberate with an ancient thrum.

"Time to choose, Marcus," Kara said. "Are you with us?"

Marcus looked between his tablet and his friends—one a woman he'd trusted with his life, now revealed as something more, and one a man with a storm brewing inside. He thought of the shadowbound soldiers, the twisted shadows, the things that should not be.

"I'm with you," he said. "God help me, I'm with you. But I expect a full explanation once we're safe. With diagrams!"

Scene 5: Thorne's Introduction

"Oh, you'll get your explanations," a deep voice like ancient thunder echoed from the shadows. "But first, you need to survive."

A figure stepped into the moonlight—a man who seemed to dwarf the ancient trees. His eyes blazed with internal fire, and the air around him shimmered with contained power. Marcus stepped back, while Zayn moved forward, dropping to one knee.

"Lord Thorne," Zayn breathed.

The giant's gaze fell on Kara's pendant, then moved to her face. A smile curved his weathered features. "So," he rumbled, "another Guardian awakens. And just in time." His eyes shifted to the base, where green light pulsed against the night sky. "The fools play with forces they cannot comprehend. They must be stopped."

The howling grew closer, and now Kara could see shapes moving through the trees—real wolves, their fur shimmering with moonlight and magic, nothing like Project Chimera's twisted creations.

Thorne raised a hand, and reality seemed to bend around them. "Come," he commanded. "Haven awaits. And you have much to learn."

The sound of pursuit grew louder—both mechanical and supernatural. Thorne turned toward the noise, his massive frame seeming to grow even larger. Waves radiated from him that made the air ripple.

"The barriers between worlds grow thinner," his voice carrying the weight of centuries. "Project Chimera's meddling threatens not just this realm, but all realms."

Marcus stared openmouthed as Thorne gestured, creating a sphere of pure energy that showed images of different worlds, each one beautiful and distinct, each one threatened by spreading corruption.

"How long have you been watching?" Understanding dawning in Kara's eyes.

"Since the first experiment," Thorne's expression darkened. "Since they first tried to create artificial Guardians through crude technology. I had hoped they would see their folly, but they push further into darkness." He turned to Zayn. "Take them to Haven. The sanctuary must be prepared. War comes on swift wings."

"But you—" Zayn started.

"I will delay them," Thorne's grin flashing like lightning in a storm cloud. "These pretenders should be reminded why Guardians were once both revered and feared."

He placed a massive hand on Kara's shoulder. "Your brother understood what was at stake. Now you must continue his work." He pressed something into her palm—an ancient coin pulsing with energy. "This will guide you to Haven. Go!"

Thorne turned to face the oncoming threat, his form blazing with a force that made the forest bow away from him. "Go now! Haven awaits, and time grows short!"

Scene 6: Journey to Haven

The coin burned in Kara's palm, projecting a path of silvery light that only they could see. They hurried through the forest, which seemed to help conceal their passage, branches parting before them and closing behind to hide their trail.

"I don't understand," Marcus panted as they ran. "Haven? Different realms? And who—what—was that back there?"

"Thorne is... was... is a legend," Zayn explained between steps, "one of the original Guardians. Some say he's as old as the barriers between worlds."

The surrounding forest changed. The trees grew more ancient, their bark shimmering with faint luminescence. Mushrooms glowed in ethereal colors, and the air felt charged with ancient magic.

"We're crossing through," Zayn said. "The veil is thinner here. Step where I step."

They navigated a path that seemed to fold through dimensions. Marcus gasped as they passed a tree that existed in multiple realities at once, its leaves falling upward in one version, burning with blue fire in another.

"The laws of physics," clutching his useless tablet like a lifeline. "They're not breaking. They're... expanding."

Kara smiled despite their situation. "Now you're starting to understand."

Scene 7: Passion

They paused in a clearing filled with luminescent flowers, pulsing in rhythm with their heartbeats. The coin from Thorne had cooled, suggesting safety, at least for the moment.

"We should rest," Zayn said. "The passage between realms is easier with a clear mind."

While Marcus sat examining a flower that changed color when he breathed near it, Kara found herself drawn to the edge of the clearing. The moons—now two of them—cast everything in a silvery-blue light that reminded her of Zayn's eyes.

She felt him approach before she heard him, his energy calling to hers like a song she'd always known but never heard.

"Shukára," he said. She turned to face him, and the world seemed to hold its breath.

"I've wanted to tell you," he began, "since that first day, there was something about you. Something I recognized, even before I knew what you were."

She stepped closer, drawn by something deeper than the physical. Their energies mingled, creating small auroras in the air around.

"I felt it too," she whispered. "I just didn't understand what I was feeling."

He brushed her hair off her face, and where his hand touched her skin, light danced between them. Their pendants pulsed in synchronized rhythm.

He placed his forehead on her forehead as if to exchange auras.

Their lips met, like worlds colliding in the gentlest way possible. The flowers blazed brighter, and for a moment, every layer of reality unfolded before them—all beautiful, all connected, each one reflected in the other's eyes.

The kiss deepened, and Kara felt as though she could sense every particle of light between the worlds, all of them dancing in celebration.

From his spot by the flowers, Marcus cleared his throat. "Um, guys? Your light show is beautiful and all, but... are we being hunted by supernatural forces or not?"

They broke apart, laughing. But their hands remained linked, bonded, with energy still flowing between them.

"Right," Kara tried to sound professional, despite her glowing smile. "Haven. We should..."

"Yes," Zayn agreed, not releasing her hand. "Haven." But the way he looked at her suggested that perhaps he'd already found his.

Scene 8: Arrival in Haven

The transition between worlds felt like stepping through a veil of liquid starlight. When their vision cleared, the sight before them drew collective gasps of wonder.

Haven unfolded before them—a sanctuary of harmony where nature and architecture melded. Homes nestled among the trees, their walls formed by living wood and stone that pulsed with a gentle luminescence. Streams of crystalline water wound through the settlement, their surfaces reflecting the iridescent glow of floating lanterns.

The air, lighter, tinged with a sweet fragrance that stirred memories of distant, forgotten joys. Trees shimmering with the diverse colors of the universes towered above them. Their branches intertwining to form a natural archway.

Zayn inhaled. "This is a place where all beings can coexist, free from the conflicts of the outside world."

Kara felt a surge of emotions—wonder and disbelief. "It's a fairy tale." She glanced at Marcus, eyes wide behind his broken glasses.

"Are we... still on Earth?" he whispered. He stared at a group of children chasing butterfly like creatures that left trails of light.

Haven sprawled across multiple levels of reality at once, a city that existed in the spaces between worlds. Crystal spires caught light from a dozen different suns, refracting it in impossible colors. Gardens floated in mid-air, their flowers blooming in four dimensions. Beings of pure energy walked alongside creatures of myth, while structures of living wood grew and shifted to accommodate their residents' needs.

"Holy quantum mechanics," Marcus breathed, his mind struggling to believe his eyes. "It's like... like every theoretical dimension decided to have a block party."

"Haven is the crossroads of realities," Zayn explained, still holding Kara's hand. "One of the few places where multiple realms touch naturally, without forcing the barriers."

A delegation approached them along a path that seemed woven from solidified moonlight. At their head walked Elder Mira, her silver hair moving in currents of energy rather than wind. The council members behind her represented species and races Kara had never imagined—some humanoid, others not.

"Welcome, young Guardians," Elder Mira's voice chimed like crystal bells. "We have awaited your—" She stopped, her opalescent eyes widening as she looked at Kara. "By the ancient light... you bear her mark. The prophecy speaks true."

The council members murmured among themselves in languages that tasted like colors and smelled like music.

"I don't understand," Kara said. "What prophecy?"

"When shadow seeks to cage the light, twins of power will ignite," Elder Mira recited. "One to learn, one to teach, until both their destinies reach."

Kara's hand tightened on her pendant. "Quin," she whispered. "He was here, wasn't he?"

"Your brother walked these paths," Elder Mira confirmed. "He learned much of what you must now learn. The council's traditional welcome must wait." Her expression grew grave. "The veilrot spreads faster than we feared. Even now, Project Chimera's twisted experiments threaten the barriers between worlds."

Above them, one of Haven's many skies darkened, showing images of Project Chimera's facilities, where sickly green energy pulsed through machines designed to pierce reality.

"Time grows short," Elder Mira continued. "You must be prepared." She gestured, and the path before them reformed, leading to a massive structure that seemed built from crystallized time. "Your training begins now. All of you," she added, including Marcus in her gaze. "Haven needs warriors of both science and spirit."

Marcus straightened, clutching his tablet. "I'll help however I can. Science at your service!"

Kara looked up at the almost incomprehensible city around them, then back at her companions—Zayn, thunderous yet protective at her side; Marcus, bewildered yet determined; and she thought of Quin, who had walked these same paths before her. She squared her shoulders and faced Elder Mira.

"We're ready," she said. "Teach us everything."

The light of a thousand realities shone down on them as they followed Elder Mira into Haven's depths. While left behind, Project Chimera's sickness continued to spread across the worlds, like ink bleeding through the pages of reality.

Scene 9: Meeting Liora the Healer

The crystalline structure opened into a vast courtyard where reality seemed to breathe. Fountains flowed upward, their waters singing ancient melodies. Gardens of healing herbs grew in geometric patterns that shifted like kaleidoscopes, each plant existing in multiple states at once—bud, bloom, and seed cycling in eternal dance.

A woman knelt beside a wounded fawn in the garden greens. Her hair rippled like liquid silver in a breeze that carried the scent of a thousand healing blooms. Light flowed from her palms into the creature, and Kara watched in amazement as the injury reversed itself, time and tissue reweaving into wholeness.

"That's impossible," Marcus whispered, then laughed. "I should stop using that word."

The fawn leaped up, now healed, and bounded away through the dimensional gardens, leaving trails of light in its wake. The healer rose, turning to face them with eyes that shimmered like opals.

"Welcome to my sanctuary," her voice carrying harmonics that made Kara's pendant resonate. "I am Liora."

"Your healing," Kara stepped forward, captivated by a strength that felt familiar yet worlds deeper than anything she'd encountered, "it's not just physical, is it?"

Liora smiled. "You have keen sight, young Guardian. True healing reaches across all layers of existence. The physical is merely the surface—beneath lie wounds of spirit, of time, of reality." She gestured to the gardens. "Every plant here exists in multiple realms at once, healing injuries that span dimensions."

Marcus had pulled out his tablet, now displaying readings unlike anything he'd seen. "The energy patterns... they're not just transferring from one point to another. They're... harmonizing? Like the universe is a symphony and you're adjusting the tune?"

"An apt metaphor," Liora approached him, studying his tablet with interest. "Science and spirit are not opposed, as Project Chimera believes. They are different languages describing the same cosmic dance." She waved her hand over his tablet, and the readings aligned into patterns that made Marcus gasp in understanding.

Turning to Kara, Liora placed her hand over the pendant.

Her eyes widened. "The Aether flow is strong in you, Shukára Vallian, like a river yearning to find its true course. You are a rare Aethermancer."

A warm sensation spread from where Liora's hand rested. Kara could see the currents of healing energy flowing through Haven—rivers of light connecting all living things.

"What does that mean?" Kara whispered, overwhelmed by the vision.

"The Aether permeates all space, all matter. Its vibrations pulse within all light, all energy. You are one with the Aether, and the Aether is one with you. You, Kara Vallian, are chosen to rise to battle the darkness, and to kneel to restore with light."

Liora's eyes grew distant. "Project Chimera's experiments have wounded reality. The barriers between worlds bleed. This gift within you—it will be crucial in the battles to come."

Zayn moved closer, protectively, but Liora smiled at him. "Fear not, Guardian. Your storms and her healing—they are two halves of the same whole. Together, you can both destroy corruption and restore the corrupted."

She led them deeper into the gardens, where other healers worked. "Here, you will learn to see beyond seeing, to heal beyond healing. All of you," she included Marcus in her gesture. "For science without spirit is as dangerous as a storm without direction."

The gardens shifted around them, revealing training areas where healers practiced their art across multiple dimensions at once. Kara felt her pendant pulse in response, recognizing ancient knowledge that seemed to awaken something deep within her soul.

"When do we begin?" she asked, watching a healer repair a tear in reality, weaving the fabric of existence back together.

Liora's smile held both warmth and warning. "You already have. Every moment here is part of your training. For when Project Chimera's perversion reaches its peak, we will need every skill, every gift, every understanding of both science and spirit to heal what they have broken."

Above them, in one of Haven's many skies, a constellation rearranged itself into the shape of Kara's pendant—a sign that even the stars recognized the path they had begun.

Scene 10: Training and Discovery

The training grounds of Haven defied conventional space and time. Multiple areas existed in the same location, each one focused on different aspects of Guardian readiness. Kara stood in the center of this dimensional overlap, her pendant pulsing with newfound awareness.

"The key," Zayn moved behind her, "is to stop thinking in terms of either/or. Reality isn't linear—it's all happening at once."

He placed his hands on her shoulders, and their energies synchronized. Through his touch, Kara could see the layers of reality he perceived—the currents flowing through Haven like rivers of light, the subtle vibrations of possibility in the air.

"Show me," she whispered.

Zayn guided her through a series of movements that seemed to fold space around them. Each gesture left trails of silver-blue energy in the air, forming patterns that reminded Kara of the designs on their pendants. As they moved together, other Guardians trained around them in overlapping realities—some appearing solid, others like ghosts, all connected.

Marcus sat cross-legged nearby, surrounded by holographic displays from his tablet, now modified by Haven's technomages to detect supernatural energies. "This is incredible," he muttered, fingers flying across multiple screens. "The energy sig natures... they're like quantum equations made visible."

Thorne's words echoed in Kara's mind: Another Guardian awakens. As if responding to her thoughts, the pendant blazed with sudden intensity. The inferno roared through her, and the training ground rippled like water.

"Careful," Zayn steadied her as the nearby Guardians turned to watch. "You're stronger than you realize."

Kara stared at her hands, now trailing wisps of silver light. "How did Quin learn to control this?"

"Perhaps this will help," a fresh voice said. Another trainer, Noni, approached carrying an ancient book that seemed to exist in multiple states—open and closed, new and ancient, all at once. "Your brother studied these texts extensively."

The book opened of its own accord, its pages filling with shifting symbols that matched those on the pendants. As Kara watched, the symbols arranged themselves into familiar patterns—training sequences, Aether flows, the fundamental language of Guardian abilities.

"It's responding to you," Noni observed with raised eyebrows. "The texts usually take weeks to attune to a new Guardian."

Kara's fingers traced the glowing symbols, and knowledge flowed into her mind like water. She saw how to shape the currents of life, guiding rather than forcing. More importantly, she understood why such force had to be wielded with wisdom.

"This is what Project Chimera doesn't understand," she said. "They try to control these forces, but it's about harmony, not dominance."

Zayn nodded. "You're beginning to think like a true Guardian."

The training continued as Haven's many suns traced their paths across multiple skies. Kara learned to channel energy through her pendant, to see the layers of reality and move between them. Zayn taught her the ancient forms of Guardian combat, where physical movement and ethereal essence flowed as one.

Marcus, meanwhile, worked with Haven's scholars to bridge the gap between science and spirit. His tablet became a window into the metaphysical, translating supernatural energies into data that revealed its secrets.

But during a brief rest, as Kara watched the ever-shifting gardens of Haven, her hand strayed to her pendant. "We're running out of time, aren't we?" she asked Zayn. "I can feel it—the veilrot spreading."

"Yes," he admitted, his eyes on the darkening skies above. "Project Chimera grows bolder. The barriers between worlds grow weaker." He took her hand, their bond creating a soft aurora around them. "But you're learning faster than anyone expected. Your connection to the Aether is extraordinary."

The pendant pulsed, and for a moment, Kara thought she felt an echo of Quin's presence—as if somewhere across the dimensions, he could feel her on his path.

Scene 11: Visions of Quin

The meditation chamber, a sphere of pure crystal, cradled Kara in a void where multiple realities intersected. Kara sat in its center, cross-legged, her pendant floating inches from her chest as she practiced the deeper aspects of Guardian meditation.

"Let your consciousness expand," Noni instructed from somewhere outside the sphere. "Don't try to find him. Let the connection that already exists guide you."

Kara breathed, letting her awareness spread through Haven's multilayered reality. The pendant's light pulsed in rhythm with her heartbeat, each wave expanding her perception further. Colors she had no names for flowed past her consciousness. Sounds that existed between moments whispered ancient secrets.

Then—something shifted.

The void around her transformed into a landscape of shadow and darkness. Green energy, sickly and wrong, pulsed through mechanical veins that seemed to grow into reality. And there, in the heart of it all...

"Quin," she whispered.

Her brother stood before a massive device, his hands gliding over controls that twisted reality like clay. But something felt off. His movements lacked their usual grace—jerky, mechanical. Project Chimera's veilrot coiled around him, vines of green lightning tightening their grip.

Yet his pendant still glowed with pure light, fighting against it.

"Shukára," his voice echoed across dimensions, strained but undefeated. "Listen carefully. They haven't broken me. Not where it matters."

She tried to move closer, but the vision kept her at a distance. "Where are you? I'll find you, I'll—"

"No!" The force of his warning made the crystal sphere resonate. "Not yet. You need to understand first. Project Chimera, they're not just trying to control. They're trying to..." The dark forces tightened around him, making him grimace. "The Heart of Worlds, Kara. Everything connects there. If they gain control of it..."

"Tell me how to help you," she pleaded.

His image faded, Project Chimera pulling him back. But his eyes met hers with fierce determination. "Learn everything you can. Trust your instincts. And Kara…" His hand touched his pendant, matching her gesture. "I left you a trail to follow. In the patterns, in the currents… when you're ready, you'll see it."

"Quin, wait!"

"Remember what she told us the night we got these pendants? 'When all realms align…'"

"'Twin Guardians will be born,'" Kara finished, tears streaming down her face.

His smile, though pained, held unwavering faith in her. "Find me when you're ready, but first, become what you were meant to be. The realms need their Guardian more than I need rescue."

The vision shattered like crystal, leaving Kara back in the meditation sphere. Her pendant dropped back to her chest, burning with renewed purpose. Outside, Zayn and Marcus waited with Noni, their faces showing concern.

"You saw him," Zayn said.

Kara stood, power swirling around her like a storm of starlight. "Yes. And now I know what we're fighting for." She faced her companions, her eyes shining with determination. "Project Chimera isn't arbitrarily destroying barriers between dimensions. They're after The Heart of Worlds."

"The Heart of…" Marcus consulted his tablet, then looked up in shock. "That's not just a legend?"

"No," Noni's face had gone pale. "It's the nexus of all realities, the one point where all realms bond and all energy flows in balance. If they gain control of it…"

"They would decimate everything," Kara finished. Her pendant pulsed with her brother's lingering presence, and with the weight of the choice before her. Save him now or become strong enough to save everything.

Zayn moved to her side, taking her hand, creating a sphere of pure light around them. "Then we'd better make sure you're ready," he said. "All of us."

Through the crystal sphere's walls, Haven's many skies had grown darker, as if the fabric of reality sensed the coming storm.

CHAPTER 5: SHADOWS OF CONFLICT

Scene 1: The Ominous Prelude

Kara jerked awake in her Haven quarters, heart pounding. In her dreams, she'd seen Haven engulfed in flames that burned with that sickly green. Warning pulses emanated from her pendant, its warmth a sharp contrast to the sudden chill in the air.

Crystal, living wood, and pure energy—the seamless architecture of her room—seemed to shiver. Reality's molecules vibrated with tension, like the moment before lightning strikes.

A deep horn blast echoed through Haven's multiple dimensions, its harmonics carrying warnings in languages older than time. Aether surged through Kara's core, propelling her forward before her conscious mind could catch up.

She met Zayn in the corridor, his silver-blue eyes already glowing. Without words, they ran toward Haven's northern watchtower, their feet barely touching the ground as they half-ran, half-flew through overlapping realities.

Marcus and Thorne had reached first, along with a dozen sentinels. Marcus's modified tablet displayed energy readings that made no sense, even in this supernatural space—reality seemed to fold in destructive patterns.

"Look," one sentinel whispered, pointing to the sky.

Dark birds circled overhead, but not natural creatures. Their wings left tears in the fabric of reality, realmscars, and their eyes burned red like coals. As they flew, they formed complex patterns against Haven's multiple suns—symbols that made Kara's pendant burn with recognition.

"Harbingers," Thorne's voice rumbled like distant thunder. "They herald potential that should not be wakened."

Kara's enhanced vision, honed by her recent training, pierced the dimensional veils. There, at the forest's edge where multiple realms overlapped, she saw them: an army of shadows and twisted light. Human soldiers in armor that pulsed with Project Chimera's toxic energy stood alongside creatures that defied description—beings of pure darkness bound by technological restraints, twisted to serve unnatural ends.

"They've done it," Marcus's tablet's screen cracking under the force of the supernatural data flooding in. "Project Chimera... they've figured out how to bind supernatural entities to their will."

"Not bind," Zayn corrected. "Torture. Those creatures... they're being forced to exist in ways that violate the fundamental laws of reality."

Thorne's massive frame seemed to grow even larger as he surveyed the gathering army. "They march on Haven," he declared. "They believe that here, where realms touch naturally, they can force open a path to The Heart of Worlds."

Kara's hand tightened on her pendant. In her mind, she saw Quin again, fighting against the energy that sought to control him. Now she understood—he existed as more than a prisoner or forced laborer. A test subject, he proved that Project Chimera could corrupt even a natural Guardian.

"We need to warn the Council," she said, turning to Thorne. "We need to gather every ally we have. This isn't just an attack on Haven—it's an assault on reality."

The Harbinger birds screamed in unison, their cry tearing holes in the sky, realmscars, through which that green disease began to seep. Haven's multiple suns seemed to dim, as if reality recoiled from the approaching force.

"Sound the general alarm," Thorne commanded. "We are the last line of defense for all reality. Haven will stand and fight! As Haven goes, so go The Realms."

As they rushed to gather Haven's defenders, Kara glimpsed something in the manufactured army that made her blood run cold—a figure in shadows that moved with horrible familiarity. Not Quin, but someone else she knew, someone who had been watching all along.

The war for reality was about to begin.

Scene 2: Rallying the Allies

Haven's Grand Hall defied conventional space, its boundaries shifting between realities as representatives from various supernatural communities filed in. The chamber expanded to accommodate each new arrival from the outskirts of Haven: proud Elves with armor that shifted like liquid starlight; Dwarven masters whose rune-etched hammers resonated with the primal force of the deep earth; Elemental lords enveloped in the essence of their domains; and dozens of other beings that Kara couldn't name.

Tension thickened the air, centuries-old rivalries simmering beneath a thin veneer of civility.

A Fire Elemental lord positioned as far as possible from a Water Sage, their energies crackling when they made eye contact.

Elder Mira gathered their attention and urged them to listen to Shukára. "Silence! Our worlds are at risk of extinction. Lend an ear to our guest, who brings critical information for all our survival."

Kara stood before them, her pendant blazing with an aura that commanded attention. She felt Zayn's reassuring presence behind her, his spirit harmonizing with hers, strengthening them both.

"I know many of you have been at odds with each other in the past," her voice carrying to every corner of the shifting space. "Some of those conflicts stretch back millennia. But what we face now threatens everything—not just Haven, but the fabric of reality."

She gestured, and her pendant projected images into the air: Project Chimera's shadowbound soldiers, the supernatural entities bound against their will, the Harbinger birds that left realmscars in the sky.

"They're not just breaking down the barriers between worlds," she continued. "They want to shatter the harmony of the realms. Those beings you saw? They're like us—creatures of magic and spirit. But Project Chimera has found ways to twist that essence, to bind it to their will through technology and torture."

A murmur ran through the crowd. An Elven queen stood, her hair moving in winds from another dimension. "Why should we trust any human? Your kind has always sought to control what they don't understand."

"Because I'm not just human," Kara's power flared, and for a moment, her true nature as a Guardian shone through, making several beings gasp. "I stand between worlds, as many of you do. And I've seen what happens when the balance is broken."

She projected another image—the army gathering at Haven's borders. "They don't distinguish between our kinds. To them, we're just subjects to be harvested, primal forces to be bent to their will. They've already taken my brother, twisted his Guardian gifts to serve their purposes. They'll do the same to any of us they catch."

"The human speaks truth," rumbled a Dwarven elder, his beard braided with gems that captured light from multiple realities. "We've felt the disease spreading through the deep regions. The stones cry out against it."

An Elemental lord made of living lightning crackled forward. "But how do we fight an enemy that turns our own abilities against us?"

"Together!" Kara's voice rang steady and unwavering. "They are used to fighting fractured souls—enemies divided within, riddled with doubt and discord. But they cannot fathom the strength born from true harmony. Our unity flows not from dominance, not from fear, but from the power of understanding and the will to uplift each other. That is our strength, and that is the force they will never conquer."

She raised her pendant, letting its pure light wash over the assembly. "Look around you. Haven exists because all our strengths coexist, complement each other... Water and Fire, Earth and Air, Light and Shadow—all parts of the greater balance. That's what Project Chimera can never understand, and that's why Project Chimera will never prevail."

The hall fell silent. Then, from the back, a massive figure came forward—Thorne, his presence commanding even in this august company.

"I have walked the realms since the first barriers were drawn," his voice rolled like thunder. "I have seen empires rise and fall, watched civilizations burn and be reborn. But never have I seen a threat like this." He strode forward to stand beside Kara. "This Guardian speaks truth. She knows the enemy. And now she knows us. United we stand, or divided we fall."

One by one, the representatives stood. The Elven queen inclined her head. The Dwarven elder raised his hammer in salute. Elements swirled in agreement. Ancient adversaries exchanged glances of respect.

"For Haven," they began to call out, their voices rising in a chorus that shook reality. "For all the realms!"

As the chorus of voices calling out for Haven began to quiet, Elder Mira stepped forward, her robes shimmering with the subtle glow of the elements she commanded. Her staff tapped the ground, sending a ripple of energy through the air. All eyes turned to her, and the room fell silent once more.

"Kara," Mira's voice was soft yet carried the weight of centuries. "You are a greenhorn to Haven, but sometimes it takes fresh eyes to see the path that others cannot. Your courage has ignited a flame in all of us. But courage alone does not lead armies—it takes wisdom, unity, and resolve." She held out her staff, the crystal atop it flaring with light. "The Staff of War shines its light on you for this battle. I name you Keeper of Haven's Unity. You shall carry the hope of all realms as our leader in this fight."

A murmur spread through the crowd as Mira extended her staff toward Kara. Tentatively, Kara reached for it, her hand trembling slightly, but as her fingers brushed the crystal, it blazed with a brilliance that momentarily filled the hall. When the light faded, Mira stepped back, a faint smile gracing her lips.

Then Thorne, towering and unyielding, stepped forward again. In his hand, he held an ancient war horn, etched with runes of power. "To lead warriors into the storm is no small burden," he said. "But I see in you the strength to bear it. I see the fire that can withstand even the shadow's coldest touch." He handed her the horn, its weight solid in her hands. "Take this, the Call of the First Guardians. With it, you will summon not just soldiers, but the spirit of Haven itself. And when you sound it, we will answer."

Kara looked at the staff in one hand and the horn in the other. The hall was still, as if every soul held their breath. She raised her gaze to meet Thorne's, then Elder Mira's. Finally, she turned to the assembly.

"I shall lead," she said, her voice steady, though her heart raced. "Not as your commander, but as one of you. Together, we will fight. Together, we will win. For Haven. For the realms!"

A roar erupted from the assembly, shaking the walls of the hall. Weapons were raised, banners unfurled, and the cry of "For Haven! For the realms!" echoed once more, this time louder, more unified, more unbreakable.

Kara felt Zayn's hand slip into hers as they watched alliances form that hadn't existed since the dawn of time. But beneath her relief, a cold certainty gripped her: Project

Chimera wouldn't wait long to attack. And somewhere within that imprisoned army, she knew, lay answers about Quin—answers that might break her heart.

Scene 3: Fortifying Haven

Haven thrummed with purpose as dozens of races worked in harmony. Elven artisans danced through the air on winds of their own making, their hands weaving spells of protection into the crystal spires. The patterns they created shimmered like frozen music, each additional layer of magic strengthening Haven's natural defenses.

Dwarven runesmiths worked below, alongside Water Sages, their combined mastery creating barriers that existed in multiple states at once—solid as mountain stone yet fluid as ocean waves. Their chants merged into a rhythm that made reality pulse in sympathy.

Marcus stood at a nexus point where ley lines crossed, surrounded by a mix of mages and technomages. His modified tablet interfaced with crystalline structures while sprites of pure energy danced around him, carrying his instructions to other teams.

"If we align the disruption field with the natural harmonic frequencies of Haven's barriers," he explained to an attentive audience, "we can create interference patterns that will blind their communications while strengthening our own."

A Fire Elemental sparked in approval. "The human understands! Magic and machine, dancing the same dance!"

Kara and Zayn moved through advanced Guardian forms in a staging area, converted from the training grounds. Their auras intertwined, creating displays of such pure energy that the other defenders stopped to watch. Kara's movements had become fluid and confident, her pendant's light forming patterns complementing Zayn's might.

"Again," she called out, her eyes shining with determination. Zayn nodded, and they began a complex sequence that looked more like a dance than combat training. Where their energies met, reality sang.

A group of young Elven warriors watched in awe as Kara demonstrated a difficult maneuver, her essence manifesting as wings of pure light. "She bridges the gap," one whispered. "Between all our kinds."

Near the central plaza, a team of ancient mages had uncovered something extraordinary—defensive runes that predated Haven. The symbols pulsed with energy that responded to Kara's presence, recognizing her Guardian essence.

"The old magics wake," an elderly mage declared. "They remember their purpose."

Kara placed her hand on the central rune, and her pendant blazed. Energy rushed through her, up into Haven's crystalline heights. A dome of pure protective force formed over the city, its surface rippling with the combined strength of all Haven's defenders.

The dome stood not only as a barrier, but as a symbol of their unity.

Elven spellcraft merged with Dwarven runes, elemental forces flowed through technological conduits, and ancient magics harmonized with new innovations. At its heart, Kara's Guardian essence acted as a keystone, binding all the different energies into a coherent whole.

Marcus looked up from his work, grinning as his instruments registered the energy levels. "Now that's what I call teamwork!"

Even those who had been skeptical of working with others found themselves caught up in the spirit of cooperation. A Shadow Walker helped a Light Weaver strengthen a complex defensive pattern. A Mountain Troll lifted a Pixie engineer to reach a high crystal that needed enhancement.

As the day progressed, Haven transformed. Its natural beauty remained, but now it bristled with defensive strength. The air hummed with protective spells, and the combined magic of dozens of races flowed through its streets like rivers of light.

Kara stood with Zayn atop one of the highest spires, watching the activity below. Their hands clasped, energy flowing between them.

"They're stronger together," she said. "We all are."

"And Project Chimera never saw this coming," Zayn smiled. "They thought they could control supernatural forces through force and division. They never understood that true strength comes from unity."

Below them, Haven shone with the light of a thousand different magics, all working as one. The coming battle would be fierce, but in this moment, watching ancient rivals work side by side, Kara felt something she hadn't expected—hope.

Scene 4: A Traitor Unveiled

Kara's pendant pulsed with warning as she walked through Haven's lower gardens. They'd finished the magical fortifications, but something felt wrong—a discordant note in Haven's symphony. Her Guardian senses, now tuned, picked up traces of anxiety and... guilt?

The source of these emotions led her to a secluded chamber beneath one of Haven's crystal spires. There, hidden by dimensional shadows, Elara stood—one of Haven's most talented empaths. Yet something felt off. Her movements lacked their usual grace.

Her hands trembled as she traced patterns in the air, creating a small portal that shimmered with that sickly green energy Kara associated with Project Chimera.

A malevolent figure appeared in the portal—more presence than form—radiating a sickening aura. "Report," it commanded in a voice that seemed to decay the air around it.

"The fortifications are complete," Elara's voice heavy with shame. "They've unified the old magics with new defenses. The Guardian—she's stronger than expected. Her power acts as a binding force, harmonizing all the different magical disciplines."

"Excellent," the figure purred. "And the weak points you created?"

Kara's heart clenched. All that work, all that unity—compromised from within.

"In place," Elara confirmed, a tear sliding down her cheek. "But please, you promised. What about my—"

"Your little family will remain unharmed, as long as you continue to cooperate." The figure leaned forward, its features illuminated by portal-light. "We're not monsters, Elara. We're visionaries. Once we control The Heart of Worlds, we can remake reality. No more suffering, no more chaos. Perfect order."

"Perfect slavery!" Kara stepped from the shadows.

Elara whirled, her eyes wide with terror. The figure in the portal shifted its attention, and Kara felt its cold interest wash over her like a toxic wave.

"Ah, the Guardian herself," it said. "How... fortunate."

"Kara, please," Elara held up her hands, tears flowing now. "They have my children. My whole family. They said they would—"

"We could have helped you," Kara spoke gently, despite her racing heart. "Haven protects its own. You only had to ask."

"Captain Samantha Reed said she would help my children become great Masters, that she wanted to help our realm, but only if I kept it secret." Elara sobbed. "I agreed. Then they captured them and threaten to torture them if I said anything. You haven't seen what they can do, what they—"

The portal flared. "Enough!" the figure commanded. "Elara, deal with her. Now!"

Elara's form blurred as she gathered her empathic strength. For a moment, Kara felt the full weight of Elara's emotional anguish—a mother's desperation, guilt, and fear all twisted together by Project Chimera's manipulation.

But before either of them could move, Zayn materialized from the shadows behind Elara. He'd been tracking Kara, sensing her concern through their shared connection.

Elara's eyes darted between them. The portal crackled with dark energy. In that frozen moment, Kara saw every outcome racing through the empath's mind.

Then Elara made her choice.

A blast of pure emotional energy exploded outward, blinding everyone. When Kara's vision cleared, Elara had vanished, leaving the lingering sensation of her guilt and fear.

The portal collapsed, but not before the dark figure's last words slithered through: "The game changes, Guardian. How will you protect them all when the barriers fall?"

"We need to warn the Council," Zayn said. "If she created weak points in our defenses—"

"Then we find them," Kara finished. "And we prove to everyone like Elara that Haven protects its own." Her pendant pulsed with renewed purpose. "Project Chimera thinks they can use our compassion and differences against us. They don't understand. Those are our greatest strengths."

They hurried toward the Council chambers, but Kara's mind raced ahead to the coming battle. Somewhere out there, Elara's family waited for rescue. Beyond them, Quin remained trapped in Project Chimera's grasp.

The real question loomed: how many other spies had Project Chimera planted? How many other families lay entangled as leverage? And how could Haven fight an enemy who twisted love into a weapon?

Scene 5: The First Assault

A stillness fell over Haven as dusk painted its multiple skies in vibrant colors, only possible in this realm. Birds of light, Haven's natural aerial sentinels, froze in mid-flight before scattering in all directions. The air seemed to hold its breath.

Kara stood atop Haven's eastern wall, Zayn beside her, as the first wave of Project Chimera's forces emerged from distorted space. That familiar sickly green light heralded their approach, infecting reality. But now, thanks to Elara's betrayal, Kara saw their method—they bypassed dimensional barriers, exploiting crafted weak points.

"Marcus," she spoke into a communication crystal. "Status of the defensive grid?"

"Working on it," his voice crackled back, strained with concentration. "Elara's sabotage was subtle. She wove the weaknesses into the fabric of our defensive spells. I'm trying to isolate—wait, something's wrong."

Before he could explain, devices activated within Project Chimera's ranks—twisted amalgamations of technology and contaminated magic. They pulsed in harmony with the weak points in Haven's barrier, creating resonance patterns that made reality shriek in protest.

The protective dome over Haven shuddered. Cracks appeared on its surface, leaking pure interdimensional energy.

"All defenders to their positions!" Kara's voice amplified by her pendant.

Around her, Haven's unified forces moved with practiced precision. Elven archers nocked starlit arrows. Dwarven shield-masters locked their runic barriers together. Elemental lords summoned their elements.

But Project Chimera had anticipated this. As their forces advanced, Kara saw the horror of what they'd created: manipulated versions of supernatural beings, bound in technological harnesses that forced their abilities to serve twisted ends. A bound Air Elemental, its pure essence tainted green, screamed as its now-controlled powers tore holes in Haven's outer defenses.

"They're using our own kind against us," an Elven commander said in horror.

"Then we free them," Kara's pendant blazing. "Remember your training! Focus on the binding devices, not our friends enslaved by them!"

The battle erupted in earnest. Haven's defenders fought with everything they had, once rivals now working in harmony. But for every being they freed, two more seemed to come. The enemy pressed forward, their devices exploiting every weakness Elara had created.

Zayn manifested a storm of pure energy, disrupting the enemy's technological components. Beside him, Kara moved through the forms she'd practiced, her Guardian abilities allowing her to bridge the gaps between different magical disciplines. Where Elven magic faltered, she reinforced it with Dwarven runes. When elemental attacks weakened, she bolstered them with pure Guardian energy.

Thorne became colossal as his Guardian energy transformed him into his Brobdingnagian ancestral form for war. As he attacked the enemy forces, the battlefield shook under his massive frame and force. He ran straight through physical and magical barriers, carving a path with little impediment, tossing the enemies high and deep as he pounded through.

Yet despite his efforts, Haven faced overwhelming forces.

The enemy had too many advantages: the element of surprise, Elara's inside knowledge, and the horrific efficiency of their massive forces.

"Kara!" Marcus's voice cut through the chaos. "The main defensive grid—it's going to collapse! The sabotage is too deep!"

She looked up at the dome of protective energy above Haven, watching cracks spread like a spiderweb across its surface. Around her, defenders fought with desperate courage, exhaustion creeping into their movements. They never expected an attack this soon.

An intense blast from the enemy lines sent Kara and Zayn staggering.

"We need to fall back," he said. "Regroup behind the secondary defenses."

"If we fall back, we lose the outer ring," Kara warned. "We need to move the refugees we promised to protect—"

Zayn's eyes met hers, filled with determination and something deeper. "This isn't the end. It's just the first battle."

"Yes, it's still acid in my throat." Kara, turning to the lines of defense. "All forces... fall back to secondary positions!" she commanded. "Orderly withdrawal! Get the civilians to the inner sanctum!"

As they executed a fighting retreat, Kara glimpsed something that made her blood run cold—that figure in the enemy ranks, watching through the chaos with familiar eyes, yet again. Not Quin, but someone else she knew from the base. Someone who'd been watching all along, waiting for this moment.

The first battle for Haven neared its end in retreat, but Kara swore it wouldn't mean defeat.

They would learn from this, adapt, become stronger. Project Chimera thought they'd struck a decisive blow, but they didn't understand what they'd done.

They'd given Haven's defenders something more potent than any magic or technology—a common enemy, and a reason to fight as one.

Scene 6: Plan of Desperation

The Council chamber buzzed with tension as Haven's defenders regrouped. War maps floated in the air, showing the enemy's position in multiple dimensions. The sickly green corruption had spread through the outer rings of Haven, turning places of natural beauty into twisted mockeries of themselves.

Casualties from the first assault filled the healing chambers. The sight of proud Elven warriors and mighty Elemental lords brought low had shaken everyone's confidence. Even the Dwarven contingent, known for their stoic nature, showed signs of worry in their furrowed brows.

"Their disruptors are the key," Marcus explained, his tablet projecting analyses of the enemy's devices. "They're not just machines—they're fusion points where perverted supernatural energy meets their vile technology. Each one acts as an anchor, forcing reality to bend to their will."

Kara studied the projections, detecting patterns. "And they're using them in concert," she added. "Each device meshed and connected with the others, creating a web of corruption, like a large net to spread the virus, that grows stronger with every pulse."

"Our conventional warfare won't work," Zayn's intense tone delivered with controlled fury. "We've seen how they can redirect our attacks, use them to strengthen their own defenses."

The Council members shifted, remembering how their strongest attacks turned against them. An Elemental lord, straight faced, wept, haunted by how his strike twisted against his own kind.

Kara's pendant pulsed as an idea formed. "What if instead of attacking the battlefield devices, we attack the control devices on their base? What if we send in a small team—people who know their technology, combined with those who understand the supernatural elements?"

"A surgical strike," Thorne rumbled. "While their attention is focused on our main forces."

"It's possible," Marcus's fingers flying over his tablet. "Their security will be concentrated on defending against large-scale magical attacks. They might not be watching for a few individuals—"

An Elven queen stood and interrupted. "It's suicide! Their forces patrol every approach. Even if you reached the base devices, disabling them would require understanding of both the technological and supernatural elements."

"Then we send people who understand both," Kara said. She turned to Marcus. "You've been studying their tech since the beginning, and now you've seen how it interacts with magic."

Marcus straightened, his mind already racing with possibilities. "With the right tools, and maybe some Dwarven runic enhancement..."

"I'm going with you," Zayn said, in a tone that brooked no argument. His power swirled around him like a contained storm. "I can help mask our approach."

Thorne stepped forward, his massive presence commanding attention. "I will accompany you as well. My knowledge of the old ways will prove useful."

A mage spoke up from the back of the chamber: "There is... a prophecy." All eyes turned to her. "It speaks of a warrior who bridges worlds, who turns the tide of darkness not through force, but through understanding. One who sees the patterns others miss."

Kara felt the weight of destiny settle on her shoulders as the mage's words resonated with her pendant. Everything—her training with Zayn, her technical discussions with Marcus, her growing ability to harmonize different magic—had prepared her for this moment.

"This is how we win!" she declared. "Not with an overwhelming number of destructive fighters, but with precision. Not with deceit, but with understanding. Not with dominion, but with harmony! We show them who we are. We show them Haven!"

The Council chamber fell silent as her words sank in. Then, one by one, the leaders nodded. They had seen her fight, watched her bring different factions together, witnessed her ability to bridge the gap between technology and magic.

Marcus pulled up schematics of the enemy's positions. "When do we leave?"

"As soon as possible," Kara replied. "Every moment we wait, this disease spreads deeper into Haven."

They prepared: charting maps, checking gear, crafting the approach. Beneath it all stirred hope—their first since the attack.

Scene 7: The Hidden Path

The ancient tunnels beneath Haven defied normal space-time, twisting through layers of reality like roots through soil. Kara led the way, her pendant's light revealing paths that existed in multiple dimensions at once. Behind her, Zayn helped stabilize the shifting reality around them, while Marcus consulted his modified tablet that combined interdimensional position locating with lidar.

Thorne brought up the rear, his massive form somehow moving with perfect silence. "These tunnels predate Haven," Thorne rumbled. "They're not just passages through space, but through the fabric of reality."

The walls pulsed with their own inner light, covered in runes that shifted and changed as they watched. Some seemed to follow them with ancient intelligence, evaluating their worth.

"Look at these readings," Marcus whispered. "The patterns in the runic sequences—they're quantum equations. It's not just magic, it's—"

"The original language of reality," Kara finished, her pendant resonating with the symbols. "The patterns that existed before the barriers between worlds were drawn."

They reached a vast chasm that seemed to drop into infinite darkness. Bridges of pure light arced across it, each one leading to a different version of the other side. The wrong choice would send them into another dimension.

Marcus's tablet could not get clear readings through the dimensional interference. "How do we know which bridge to take?"

Kara studied the paths, remembering her training. "We don't choose with our minds. We feel it." She closed her eyes, letting her Guardian senses expand. The pendant grew warm, pulling her toward one particular bridge that shimmered with familiar energy.

As they crossed, the bridge became solid beneath their feet, responding to their combined purpose. But halfway across, they encountered their first real challenge—an ancient door covered in complex runes, sealed for millennia.

Thorne stepped closer. "The Gate of Truth. It requires more than sheer force to open."

Kara approached the door, studying the runes. They reminded her of the patterns in her pendant, but more complex, shifting in ways that made her eyes hurt if she looked too long.

"It's a puzzle," she realized. "Not just in one dimension, but in all of them."

She reached out, letting her pendant's light illuminate the runes. The patterns moved faster, aligning and realigning in complex sequences. Kara closed her eyes and focused on the Aether flowing through her, allowing her to see not just the physical symbols of the runes, but the currents running through them.

"Here," she traced a pattern in the air. "It's not about solving each layer. It's about finding the one pattern that works across all dimensions at once."

Her fingers moved with increasing confidence, weaving a solution that existed in multiple states. The door responded, its runes beginning to harmonize with her pendant's energy.

The air thickened, and a spectral figure materialized—a guardian spirit of the ancient paths. Its form shifted between different aspects of reality, both beautiful and terrifying.

"Who seeks passage through the Realmbridge?" it asked in a voice that echoed through dimensions.

Kara stepped forward. "We do."

"And what would you give to stop the darkness that spreads above?"

"Whatever it takes," she replied without hesitation.

The spirit's gaze pierced through her, seeing past physical form to the essence of her being. "Even if the cost is everything you believe to be true about yourself?"

Kara thought of Haven under siege, of manipulated beings forced to fight their own kind, of Quin somewhere in the enemy's ranks. "Truth isn't what we believe," she said. "It's what we choose to become when faced with darkness."

The spirit seemed to smile—a gesture that rippled through space and time. It raised its hand, and a glowing pendant materialized, similar to her own but ancient beyond measure.

"Take this, Aethermancer," it said. "When the moment comes, you'll know how to use it. But remember—true power lies not in what we can do, but in what we choose not to do when we could."

The spirit faded, leaving the pendant floating in the air. As Kara took it, she felt it harmonizing with her, adding another layer to her understanding of these new forces.

The door swung open, revealing the continuation of their path. They moved with renewed purpose, knowing they journeyed toward more than battlefield positioning—they journeyed toward the knowledge of how to wield great power.

The ancient tunnel's exit shimmered like a heat mirage as Kara led her team toward their final approach. But something felt different—the two pendants resonated together, creating harmonics that made her skin tingle. The ancient one pulsed with a rhythm that seemed to call to something deep within her Guardian essence.

"Wait," holding up her hand. The others froze as she closed her eyes, focusing on the strange, unfamiliar sensation.

The pendants' energies spiraled together. Her awareness expanded in a way she'd never experienced. She could see the layers of reality like pages in a book, but now—she could reach out and turn those pages.

"Kara?" Zayn's concerned voice seemed to come from far away. "Your eyes..."

"They're shifting through different realities," Marcus breathed, his tablet's sensors going wild. "Like she's existing in all of them at once."

Through her enhanced perception, Kara saw the enemy camp layered through multiple dimensions. But more than that, she saw the spaces between those dimensions—blind spots where reality hadn't quite decided which version of itself to be.

"I can hide us," her voice carrying ethereal overtones. "Not in shadow, not in light, but in the spaces between moments."

Thorne's eyes widened with recognition. "The Twilight Walk. A Guardian art thought lost for millennia. The ability to guide others through the spaces between realities."

Kara reached out, causing the combined energies of both pendants to envelop her companions. It felt like drawing a veil of possibility around them—not quite invisible, but existing out of sync with any single reality.

"Don't let go of each other," she instructed. "We'll be walking through the seams of existence."

They emerged from the tunnel into the enemy camp, but now they moved like ghosts through the spaces between seconds. Project Chimera's forces looked right through them, their corrupted sensors scanning realities but missing the spaces between them.

Through her enhanced vision, Kara could see everything: the weak points in the enemy's defenses, the trapped supernatural beings fueling their devices, even the strands of veilrot spreading through reality. But most importantly, she saw the paths between it all—safe routes through the chaos that shouldn't exist, but did.

Marcus watched through his tablet as reality shifted around them. "This is incredible. You're not just hiding us, you're... we're quantum tunneling through probability."

A patrol of guards passed within inches of them, their twisted energy making the air shimmer with that sickly green light. But in this state, walking the Twilight Path, even their corruption couldn't touch what didn't quite exist.

Kara felt the power humming through her, demanding perfect control. One slip and they'd snap back into normal space-time, scattered across multiple realities. But something about it felt natural and predestined.

"The disruptors are ahead," her voice still carrying those strange harmonics. "I can see how they're anchored to reality. And..." seeing something that made her heart skip, "I can see the prisoners they're draining."

Through the layered realities, she glimpsed familiar faces among the captives—including members of Elara's family. Now she understood why turning off the devices wouldn't be enough.

They would have to save everyone.

Scene 8: Camp Infiltration & Quin

Still walking the Twilight Path between realities, Kara guided her team closer to the prisoner compounds. Through her enhanced vision, the scene unfolded as a nightmare of layered truths—vile energy coursed through technological veins, prisoners' natural essence siphoned into the disruptors, and reality groaned under the strain.

"Thorne," she whispered through the spaces between moments, "can you create a diversion on the far side of the camp?"

The ancient Guardian nodded, understanding. "Project Chimera fears what it cannot control. I'll give them chaos itself to wrestle with."

As Thorne slipped away through the quantum shadows, Kara's dual pendants pulsed with recognition. Through the layered realities, she saw him—Quin, strapped into a central device that pulsed with sickly green light. Yet something felt different about him. His pendant blazed with defiant light, battling against the green disease that fought to claim him.

"There," she breathed, her heart racing. "He's being used as some kind of focal point. His Guardian powers... they're using him to stabilize their entire network."

Zayn's hand tightened on hers. "That's why they wanted him. A natural Guardian, providing a template for their shadowbound versions."

Marcus studied the readings on his tablet. "The neural interface they're using... it's not just controlling him, it's learning from him. Every moment he resists teaches their system new ways to corrupt."

A distant explosion rocked the camp—Thorne's diversion beginning. Guards rushed toward the disturbance, their sickly auras leaving trails of twisted reality in their wake. But through her enhanced perception, Kara saw something that made her blood run cold.

"They're not all fooled," she warned. "Some of them are still watching, existing out of phase... they can almost see us."

As if to confirm her words, a nearby guard turned, its eyes sliding through multiple realities at once. For a moment, its gaze passed through the quantum spaces where they hid.

Kara made a split-second decision. She let the Twilight Walk fade just enough, bringing them into normal space-time. "Now!" she commanded. "While they're divided!"

They burst into action. Zayn exploded his stormforge outward, disrupting the technological components of the nearest devices. Marcus interfaced his tablet with a control panel, his fingers flying as he fought against the system's nefarious programming.

Kara ran toward Quin, her dual pendants blazing. Guardian energy met veilrot energy in a cascade of reality-bending forces. The air seemed to crack under the strain.

"Kara?" Quin's voice, weak but uncorrupted. His eyes focused on her through the pain. "You found me... but you don't understand... this isn't just about me. They're using us to find—"

An alarm shrieked across dimensions. Reality rippled as reinforcements phased in from other sectors. Kara moved without hesitation, newfound power flowing through both pendants. She reached out, not just with force but with understanding, seeing how the corruption had woven itself around her brother's essence.

"I'm getting you out," she promised, her hands moving through complex patterns as she worked to untangle him from the machine.

"No," he gasped. "You have to know... Project Chimera, they're not just trying to control their prisoners. They found something. The Heart... it's not what we thought. It's—"

A blast of dark energy cut him off, forcing them all to duck. Through the chaos, Kara heard Marcus shout, "More incoming! They're converging on our position!"

The battle for Quin's freedom—and the truth he carried—was about to begin.

Scene 9: Quin Rescue Mission

Shadowbound guards poured in from all directions, their forms flickering between realities as they phased through dimensional barriers. Thorne's diversion had drawn many away, but elite guards remained—creatures twisted by Project Chimera into perfect weapons.

As Kara fought to free Quin from the machine, a surge of sickly energy lashed out, nearly overwhelming her defenses. But at that crucial moment, her brother's pendant synchronized with her two, creating a triad of Guardian light.

Time seemed to slow as new awareness flooded through her. The three pendants resonated together. Kara could see not just the layers of reality, but the threads that bound them together. More than that—she could reach out and pluck those threads like harp strings.

"Impossible," one of the manipulated guards whispered, its twisted essence recoiling. "She's manifesting harmony."

Kara moved without thinking, her hands weaving patterns in the air that sang across dimensions. Each gesture plucked at different threads of reality, creating cascading harmonies. Where the notes touched the infected guards, their twisted bonds unraveled.

"Marcus!" her voice carrying otherworldly overtones. "The frequency—can you amplify it?"

Marcus's fingers flew across his tablet, now connected to the facility's own systems. "Broadcasting through their network... now!"

The harmonics amplified, spreading through the compound. Manipulated beings dropped to their knees as the music of perfect harmony washed over them, breaking Project Chimera's hold. The sickly green energy began to dissolve, unable to maintain its corruption in the face of perfect natural harmony.

Zayn moved like lightning through the chaos, adding thunder to Kara's symphony. Together, they created a devastating duet of purifying energy that swept through the ranks of shadowbound guards.

"The binding matrix," Quin pushed as Kara worked to free him. "It's weakening. But be careful—the feedback—"

A massive surge of corruption pushed back against the harmony, creating a discordant shriek that made reality shudder. The machine holding Quin began to overload, green lightning crackling across its surface.

"If that device explodes with him still connected," Marcus warned, "the quantum backlash could tear him apart across multiple dimensions!"

Kara refused to accept that. Focusing on the three synchronized pendants, she sang—not with her voice, but with pure Guardian energy. The song wove through layers of reality, seeking the natural resonance of every being, every particle, every quantum possibility.

The veilrot energy tried to resist, but it couldn't fight against the fundamental harmony of existence. One by one, the binding restraints dissolved.

Quin fell forward into her arms, weakened but free. His own pendant blazed with renewed strength as the rot fell away from him.

"Sister," managing a weak smile. "You've learned so much."

"Save your strength," she replied, supporting him as Zayn cleared them a path through the chaos. "We're getting you out of here."

But even as they began their retreat, alarms blared across multiple dimensions. Kara's heightened senses prickled as an overwhelming sickness drew near—a presence she had hoped to avoid a little while longer.

"Run!" Quin urged, alert despite his weakness. "She's coming—Captain Reed. What they did to her... what she chose to become..."

The air seemed to decay as a figure approached through the dimensional storm, trailing veilrot like a toxic wake.

Scene 10: Confronting Captain Reed

Reality crackled and split as Captain Reed emerged from the dimensional distortion, both familiar and horrifically transformed. Her military uniform had transformed into a twisted amalgamation of technological armor and crystallized corruption. Veins of green energy pulsed beneath her skin, and her eyes blazed with an unnatural force.

"Specialist Vallian." Reed's voice resonated across multiple frequencies, a smile twisting her features. "Or should I say, Guardian? Did you think we didn't plan for this? That we didn't want you to come?"

The harmonics from Kara's pendants wavered as the veilrot around Reed fought against natural resonance. Even the Twilight spaces between realities seemed to recoil from her presence.

"What did you do to yourself?" Kara asked, positioning herself between Reed and her weakened brother.

"I evolved," Reed spread her arms, veilrot energy cascading off her like toxic rain. "Project Chimera offered me what the military never could—true power. The ability to reshape reality." Her gaze fixed on Quin. "Your brother understood, at first. Until his Guardian nature made him resist progress."

"You mean resist becoming a monster?" Quin spat, though the effort made him sway.

Reed laughed, the sound distorting in space and time. "Monster? No. We are visionaries. The Heart of Worlds is meant to be controlled, its power harnessed for order. Join us, Kara. Join your brother and let's reshape this world!"

"This is your plan?" Kara's pendants pulsed as understanding dawned. "You can't get there without me, and you want me to lead you to Haven, to The Heart?"

"You've always been so predictable." Reed's smile turned predatory. "Your dedication to family, your need to save everyone... such useful traits to exploit."

Reed raised her hand, and reality bent around them. The harmonics Kara had been maintaining dissolved under waves of corruption. Freed guards convulsed as the sickly forces tried to reclaim them.

But something new stirred within the pendants. The third one—the ancient artifact from the guardian spirit—pulsed with a different rhythm. It didn't fight the veilrot; instead, it turned it and redirected it, revealing how corruption could transform back into pure power.

Understanding blazed through her mind. Reed hadn't just shadowbound herself; she'd created a conduit. And conduits could be reversed.

"Now!" Kara commanded.

Zayn surged forward as Marcus activated something on his tablet. The pendants blazed in perfect synchronization as Kara wove a different harmony—one that didn't fight veilrot but transformed it.

Reed's confident smile faltered as her corrupt energy flowed backward.

"What... what are you doing?" Reed's voice cracked across dimensions.

"Showing you real power," Kara's pendants creating a purifying symphony. "The power of restoration."

Reed did not relinquish. With a scream of rage, she activated a device using controls in her armor. A modified portal device pulsed with catastrophic energy.

"If I can't have The Heart," she snarled, "no one will. This device will release enough venal energy to tear reality apart!"

The device hummed with increasing intensity as Reed vanished into a dimensional rift, her last words echoing: "Find me when you're ready to embrace true destiny!"

The device ticked moments from detonation, reality already beginning to fracture around them, and no clear path to escape.

Scene 11: The Sacrifice

The modified portal device pulsed with increasing intensity, reality fracturing around it like splintering glass. Through her enhanced perception, Kara could see the damage spreading across dimensions—cracks in the fabric of existence.

"We have to shut it down," Marcus shouted over the dimensional chaos, his tablet's readings spinning out of control. "The veilrot is reaching critical mass!"

Quin pushed himself away from Kara's supporting grip, stumbling toward the device. His face, set with grim determination.

"The portal core," his voice projecting stronger now. "It's like the one they used to bind me. I understand its architecture. I can… I can reverse the flow."

"No!" Kara moved to stop him, but Quin held up his hand, creating a barrier of pure Guardian energy between them.

"Listen to me, sister," his eyes met hers with fierce intensity. "This is why I let them take me, why I studied their technology from the inside. I knew someone would have to understand it to stop it."

"There has to be another way," Kara pressed against the barrier, her pendants resonating. "We just got you back!"

"You're needed elsewhere," Quin said. "Haven, The Heart of Worlds—they need their Guardian. And now…" he smiled, touching his own pendant, "now you have the harmony, something they never understood."

The device's whine reached a fever pitch. Reality began to warp, pulling apart at the seams.

"Quin, please," Kara's voice broke. "Don't do this."

"I learned something while they held me." Already moving toward the device's core. "True power isn't in controlling reality." His hands glowed with pure Guardian energy. "It's in being willing to sacrifice everything to protect it."

Before anyone could stop him, Quin plunged his hands into the portal core. Sheer Guardian energy met veilrot energy in a cascade of blinding light. His pendant blazed as the pure energy and the venal energy clashed. He drew the corruption towards him as he entered the portal.

"NO!" Kara screamed, but Zayn held her back.

"Trust him," Zayn whispered. "He knows what he's doing."

Quin's form blurred as the energies of the portal and of Quin intertwined. The air filled with harmonics as he turned destruction into transformation.

"Remember what she told us," Quin's voice came from everywhere and nowhere, his form becoming pure light. "'Twin Guardians will be born.' You're the protector they need, Kara. The Guardian who can unite them all."

The device's catastrophic energy faded, as did Quin. Reality stabilized, and the cracks healed themselves.

A final surge of light erupted from the core. When it faded, Quin had vanished. The device lay dark and inert, its infestation neutralized.

But something glimmered in the air where Quin had stood—a subtle distortion in reality, like a door left ajar.

Marcus studied the readings. "He's not dead. These quantum signatures... he's not gone, he's just... somewhere else. Somewhere between realities."

Kara touched her pendants, and for a moment, she felt it too—an echo of Quin's presence, distant but undiminished. Not destroyed, but transformed. Waiting.

"We'll find him," Zayn promised, his hand finding hers. "But first, we honor his sacrifice by protecting what he saved."

Through her tears, Kara nodded. Haven needed them. The war against Project Chimera raged on. And somewhere out there, her brother waited to be found, again.

Scene 12: The Battle Turns

With Quin's sacrifice neutralizing the corrupted portal, a wave of pure Guardian energy rippled across dimensions, washing over Haven like the first light of dawn. The green rot dissolved wherever it touched, and reality seemed to sigh with relief.

Ancient horns sounded from Haven's highest towers—not the desperate call to arms from before, but a triumphant melody that sang of hope restored. Elven songweavers added their voices, creating harmonies that made the air shimmer with renewed vigor. Young sprites danced through the air, trailing sparkles of pure light that burned away lingering shadows.

"Look!" A young Dwarven warrior shouted, pointing to where the enemy lines had been. "The barriers!"

The infected forces' hold on reality crumbled. Without their disruptors, without the anchor of Quin, their unnatural bonds released. Beings they had enslaved broke free, their natural abilities returning in magnificent bursts of pure energy.

Elementals soared into the sky, their true forms restored, creating a spectacle that drew cheers from Haven's defenders. Fire danced with Wind, Water spiraled with Earth, and the foundations of reality sang with freedom restored.

Kara stood atop Haven's walls, watching the fireworks of victory in the valley below, her pendants blazing with pure light. The harmony she had discovered flowed out from her in waves, helping to break the last shadowbound bonds. Zayn stood beside her, his quiet storm adding strength to her melody.

Winged beings—Valkyries and Air Spirits held back by Project Chimera's veil-rot—swept through the skies, their battle cries turning into songs of victory. Young apprentice mages watched in awe, pointing and cheering as natural magic returned to the world in all its glory.

"For Haven!" The cry went up, echoing across dimensions. "For Haven!"

Marcus's modified sensors showed reality, healing, and nature reasserting itself with joyous enthusiasm. Magical creatures hidden by the corruption emerged to celebrate—phoenixes soared overhead trailing flames of rebirth, while ground dragons stamped their feet in rhythmic celebration, sending harmonious tremors through the earth.

Crystal spires that had been darkened by veilrot now blazed with internal light again. Gardens that had withered burst back into bloom, their flowers opening in every color. Young sprite children darted among the blossoms, their laughter carrying healing magic of its own.

From the refugee quarters came sounds of celebration as families reunited with those freed. The air filled with songs in a hundred different languages, all singing the same song of freedom and hope.

"The tide has turned," Thorne's voice boomed across the celebration, "but not just by force of arms. It turned because one Guardian showed us that true power lies in sacrifice and love."

Kara felt tears on her cheeks, but now she felt tears of both joy and determination. Through her enhanced senses, she could still feel that echo of Quin—not gone, but transformed, waiting to be found. His sacrifice had shown them all what real strength looked like.

A group of young magical beings approached her, their eyes shining with hope and admiration. One small sprite girl offered her a crown woven from flowers that bloomed in multiple realities across space and time.

"Tell us about him," the children begged. "Tell us about the Guardian who helped save us all!"

Kara knelt down among them, her pendants glowing. "Let me tell you about my brother, Quin," she began, "and about how love can turn even the darkest tide..."

Above them, Haven's many suns seemed to shine brighter, and reality hummed with renewed harmony. They won this battle. They dealt Project Chimera a decisive blow.

But even in victory, Kara knew this marked only the beginning. Bigger battles awaited, fiercer challenges lay ahead. Yet now, they faced them together, stronger than ever, their hearts beating in harmony with the pulse of existence.

Scene 13: The Aftermath

As the initial euphoria of victory settled into something deeper, Haven hummed with renewed purpose. The city seemed to glow from within, its crystal spires and living architecture resonating again. But beneath the celebration lay the solemn task of healing and rebuilding.

Liora moved among the wounded, surrounded by the healing gardens, her silver hair flowing like liquid moonlight. Other healers worked beside her, combining to create auroras of restorative energy. Those touched by veilrot required special care—their essence needed to be realigned with natural reality.

Kara walked among them, her pendants now working in perfect harmony. Where she passed, the healing energies grew stronger, the pure resonance of her essence helping to restore natural balance. Many reached out to touch her robes as she passed, whispering thanks not just for the victory, but for the return of hope.

"The young ones call you 'Light-Bringer' now," Zayn pressed his cheek to her cheek. "The sprite children have composed songs about how you turned darkness into harmony."

A small smile touched her lips, though her eyes held a depth of both joy and sorrow. "They should be singing about Quin. About all those who sacrificed."

As if in answer to her words, ethereal music floated through Haven's many levels. Elven voice-weavers had begun the Song of Remembrance—a melody, honoring both the lost and the transformed. The song carried tales of courage, of sacrifice, of love strong enough to turn back corruption.

Near the outer walls, Marcus worked with a team of Dwarven runesmiths and technomages, analyzing the remnants of Project Chimera's devices. His tablet now interfaced with magical sensors, bridging the gap between science and supernatural in ways that would have seemed impossible just days ago.

"Look at this," he called as Kara approached. "The veilrot didn't just break down—it transformed. Whatever Quin did, he didn't just stop the energy, he changed its fundamental nature." His eyes shone with scientific wonder. "It's like he rewrote the code of reality."

Kara touched one of the transformed devices. Through her enhanced senses, she could feel traces of her brother's essence—not destroyed, but scattered across dimensions, seeded like stardust through the fabric of reality.

"He's still out there," she said with quiet certainty. "And he left us a map to follow, hidden in the patterns of transformation."

Thorne appeared, his massive form moving silently despite his size. "The Council gathers," he announced. "There are decisions to be made about what comes next. Project Chimera is wounded, but not destroyed. And there are other, greater threats moving in the shadows."

Before they could respond, a commotion arose from the refugee quarters. A group of former prisoners, now freed from corruption, approached with urgent news.

"There are more facilities," one of them reported, her eyes still haunted by what she had seen. "Project Chimera has spread further than anyone realized. They've built their sickness into the foundations of multiple realms."

"Then we'll root it out," Kara pendants pulsing with renewed purpose. "All of it. And we'll help heal every reality they've touched."

The setting suns cast long shadows across Haven, but now those shadows held no terror. They formed just another part of the natural balance, as essential as light. Above, in one of Haven's many skies, new constellations took shape—stars rearranging themselves to tell the story of this day, this battle, this turning point.

"The war isn't over," Zayn observed, watching the stars shift.

"No," Kara agreed, taking his hand. Their combined power created a soft aurora around them. "But now we know how to fight it. Not just with force, but with harmony. With understanding. With love."

Around them, Haven continued its work of healing and preparation. They all knew this victory, magnificent as it felt, marked the start of a larger struggle—one that would determine the fate not just of their world, but of all realities.

Scene 14: Visions of the Greater Threat

Haven transformed its Council chamber. Its crystalline walls blazed with maps of multiple realms. Each map showed Project Chimera's influence spreading like dark veins through the foundations of different worlds. Kara stood before the assembled leaders, her pendants casting shadows that seemed to move with purpose across the strategic displays.

"Our victory was significant," she began, her voice carrying to every corner, "but it revealed something worse. Project Chimera isn't just corrupting our world—they're embedding their technology into the fabric of multiple realms."

Marcus stepped forward, his tablet projecting complex data patterns into the air. "They've created a network," he explained, pointing to interconnected nodes of corruption. "Each facility strengthens the others. When we freed this sector," he highlighted their recent battlefield, "we discovered at least twelve more major installations."

A murmur of concern rippled through the assembled leaders. An Elven queen rose, her form shimming with starlight. "This corruption of which you speak, spreading in a web. It is the Twilight Fall, when an entire realm plunges into darkness. How did they spread so far without the Council of Realms noticing?"

Elara, who had returned to Haven seeking redemption, stepped from the shadows. "Because they use our own fears against us," she said. "They approach each realm, offering solutions to unique problems. To war-torn worlds, they promise peace through control. To dying realms, they offer technological salvation—again through control."

"And to proud realms," Kara added, understanding dawning, "they whisper about might and superiority—through control. Each realm thinks they're getting a unique advantage, never realizing they're all being coerced into a Twilight Fall by the same force. And they are made to fear and to distrust the others with lies and false tales. Then each realm turns a blind eye to the evils of Project Chimera."

The air in the chamber grew thick with tension as leaders recognized how Project Chimera may have manipulated their own realms. But rather than discord, this revelation seemed to strengthen their resolve.

Kara's pendants pulsed with urgent energy. The maps before them blurred and transformed, showing something far more terrifying—a massive army gathering across multiple dimensions. Warriors manipulated by Project Chimera's influence, but now united under a single banner.

"They're mobilizing," Thorne's ancient eyes narrowed, "not just their technology, but entire armies."

Through her enhanced senses, Kara saw more than just the army—she saw waves of future possibility radiating from this moment. "They're going to attack the Guardians," she announced, her voice heavy with certainty. "If they can distract them in their homelands, they eliminate the forces that could resist in the battle for The Heart of Worlds."

The visions flowed faster now, showing battles erupting across countless realities. But something else caught her attention—a pattern hidden within the chaos, a familiar energy signature that made her pendants resonate with recognition.

"Quin knew," she breathed. "He saw this coming. That's why he walked into that portal of veilrot. He's positioning himself to help us fight back!"

The Council chamber erupted in urgent discussion as leaders began forming battle plans. But Kara held up her hand for silence, her pendants blazing with purpose.

"We don't just need armies," she declared. "We need unity like never before. Project Chimera expects us to fight realm by realm. Instead, we create something new—an Inter-Realm Council, with a mandate to coordinate across all dimensions."

"Impossible," someone protested. "The logistics alone—"

"Are already solved," Marcus interrupted, his tablet displaying new configurations. "Haven's crystal matrix can be modified to maintain constant communication across all allied realms. We can coordinate in real-time, share resources, combine different forms of magic and technology in ways they'll never expect."

One by one, the leaders nodded. Former rivals planned joint strategies, shared former guarded secrets. Faced with annihilation, former boundaries dissolved.

Energized by their unity, Kara declared, "No longer will we fight in scarcity. Instead, we will thrive in abundance. Together, we will ensure all our victories!"

"Send the call," Kara commanded, her voice ringing with authority that surprised even her. "To every allied realm, every free people, every being who chooses harmony over corruption. The time has come to stand together."

Above them, Haven's many skies rippled with anticipation. The war for reality comes.

Scene 15: A New Quest Begins

Haven's central plaza buzzed with dual purposes—assembling a grand army and preparing a smaller infiltration squadron.

On one side, military leaders from dozens of realms coordinated their forces. The Dwarven War-Chief's deep voice mixed with the melodic commands of the Elven Captains as they organized their combined troops. Elemental lords taught their battle-techniques to eager recruits from other realms, while technomages worked to enhance traditional weapons with new innovations.

Meanwhile, Kara stood with her core team—Zayn, Marcus, and a select group of allies chosen for their unique abilities. The ancient pendant she'd received in the tunnels projected a map unlike any other—a living diagram of reality, showing paths between realms that led to The Heart of Worlds.

"The military council will handle Project Chimera's armies," Thorne said, his massive form casting multiple shadows in Haven's many lights. "But The Heart must be protected. If they seize it while their shadowbound forces keep us occupied..."

"They won't," Kara replied with quiet certainty. Her pendants hummed in harmony, and the map shifted, revealing hidden routes through the dimensions. "Quin left us breadcrumbs—quantum signatures scattered across reality. They'll guide us to The Heart while pointing us toward Project Chimera's weaknesses."

Marcus studied the readings on his tablet, which now interfaced with magical energies. "These paths... they're like cosmic ley lines, but they exist between realities rather than just through them. Your brother's transformation didn't just save Haven—it created a network we can follow!"

Zayn stepped closer to Kara, their energies synchronizing. "We'll need to move fast. Once Project Chimera realizes what we're doing..."

"Which is why we leave now," Kara nodded. She turned to address both groups—the military council and her expedition team. "Haven stands ready. The armies of all realms unite against veilrot. But the true battle, the fight for The Heart of Worlds, begins with us finding it."

The pendant from the Guardian of The Gate of Truth blazed with more energy, projecting images of their path ahead. They saw glittering crystal cities suspended in starlight, forests that grew through time, oceans that sang with ancient beauty, and mountains that touched multiple realms at once.

"Your journey will not be easy," Thorne warned. "Project Chimera has agents in every realm, and not all who seem friendly will be allies."

As if in answer, a haunting howl echoed through Haven's many dimensions—that same call Kara had heard so many times before. But now she understood it as more than a warning. She understood it as a call to destiny.

"Remember," Thorne's voice carried the weight of ages, "Project Chimera is just a pawn. Even they answer to a greater shadow, one that has waited millennia to bound The Heart."

The military preparations continued behind them as Kara and her team made their final preparations. Each member carried something unique: Marcus with his enhanced technology, Zayn an experienced Guardian, and others with abilities chosen for this quest.

"The armies will move to engage Project Chimera's forces," a High General announced. "While they focus on us..."

"We find The Heart," Kara finished. Her pendants pulsed with purpose, and for a moment, she felt Quin's presence scattered through reality, waiting to help guide their way.

As they prepared to step through the first portal, a young sprite child darted forward, pressing something into Kara's hand—a crystal that sang with pure, aetheric energy. "For hope," the child whispered.

Kara looked back at Haven one last time, seeing all they had built together—all they fought to protect. Then she faced forward, toward the first of many realities they would need to cross.

"For all realms," she whispered, and stepped into the light of another world.

Behind them, Haven's armies began their preparations for war, while ahead lay the greatest quest of all—a journey to the Heart of existence, with the fate of all realities hanging in the balance.

The ancient wolf's howl echoed once more across dimensions, both a warning and a blessing, as reality seemed to hold its breath, waiting to see what would unfold.

CHAPTER 6: BEYOND THE VEIL

Scene 1: The Portal to Realms Unknown

The ancient stone circle in Haven's deepest garden thrummed with potential energy. Runes carved into its weathered surface glowed as Kara approached with her team. Her two pendants—her original and the ancient one from the guardian spirit—pulsed with the circle's rhythm.

Zayn stood at her right, his storm-force crackling just beneath the surface. Marcus stood at her left, his modified tablet displaying readings that made his eyes widen with each new scan. Behind them, their chosen companions waited: Noni the spellweaver, whose magic could bridge dimensional gaps; Keairra, a shadow-walker who could navigate the spaces between realities; and Caid, an elemental harmonist who could stabilize unstable dimensional passages.

"The first portal has placed us on the edge of Haven in this hidden ancient space. From here, our journey begins. The map shows our next destination," Kara said, holding up the ancient pendant. Its light projected a path through multiple layers of reality—a route that seemed to twist through the fabric of existence. "The Ethereal City."

Thorne stepped forward, his massive form casting multiple shadows in the garden's strange light. "The ancients stir," he rumbled, placing his hand on the stone circle. Ancestral words flowed from him—not just sounds, but pure vibrational energy that made reality resonate.

As the chant built, Kara felt a familiar presence brush against her consciousness. A vision flashed through her mind—Quin, alive, in a realm of crystalline light. His pendant blazed as he looked at her through the vision.

"Trust your instincts," his voice echoed in her mind. "I left signs for you to follow, sister. Find me when the time is right, but first—"

The vision faded as the stone circle erupted with light. A portal spiraled open, its edges shimmering with the purest of light.

"What!" Marcus exclaimed, staring at his readings. "Was that like vocal recognition? The vibrations of Thorne's voice—they created repeat quantum harmonic patterns."

"Almost my scientist friend. Almost. The first of the seven gates to The Heart of Worlds awaits. Guardian Speed, my friends!" Thorne wished them well, smiling at Marcus's nonstop curiosity.

Zayn's hand found Shukára's hand, their combination creating small auroras in the air. "Ready?" he asked.

Kara looked back at Haven one last time, seeing the armies preparing for war, the combined forces of multiple realms united against corruption. Then she faced the portal, her pendants blazing with purpose.

"For all realms," she said, and stepped into the swirling vortex of light.

Reality twisted around them as they passed between dimensions. Through her enhanced senses, Kara saw layers of existence peeling away like pages in an infinite book. And somewhere, beyond the boundaries of normal space-time, she felt her brother waiting—not scattered, but transformed, holding vital knowledge they would need to protect The Heart of Worlds.

The journey to find him and the journey to save all realms, had begun.

Scene 2: Arrival in the Ethereal City

The Ethereal City materialized around them like a dream taking solid form. Towers of living crystal spiraled high, their surfaces catching light from a dozen different suns. Streets made of solidified starlight wound between buildings that seemed to exist in multiple moments of time. Celestial beings with wings of pure energy soared between the spires, leaving trails of light that formed complex mathematical patterns in the air.

"It's... it's perfect," Marcus breathed, his tablet struggling to process the readings. "The quantum coherence, the dimensional stability."

A figure descended toward them, moving with impossible grace. Her form, composed of light, given purpose, her wings trailing stardust. As she landed, the air shimmered with the brilliance of a thousand stars.

"Welcome to the Ethereal City," her voice carrying harmonics that made both Kara and Zayn's pendants resonate. "I am Shani, High Guardian of the Celestial Realm. We have awaited your arrival."

She studied them with eyes that held the depth of galaxies. "Ah," she smiled, focusing on Kara and Zayn. "The celestial bloodline runs strong in both of you. Though you've barely touched your true potential."

"Our true potential?" Zayn asked, his storm-like energy responding to her presence.

Shani raised her hand, and reality shifted around them. Kara could see threads of pure celestial energy running through her own being, through Zayn's, connecting them to the fabric of existence.

"Your Guardian powers are not just abilities," Shani explained. "They are echoes of the original force that shaped reality. Watch closely."

She moved her hands in an intricate pattern, and the space between them began to glow. It projected more than light. It projected a pure creative energy, the same energy that had first sparked existence into being.

"Together," she instructed them. "Let your essence merge not just in harmony, but in creation."

Kara and Zayn faced each other, their pendants pulsing in sync. As their energies combined, something new happened. Instead of just harmonizing, they wove together, forming patterns that wrote themselves into reality.

"Yes," Shani's voice rising. "You're not just Guardians of what exists—you are shapers of what could be. Creation flows through your celestial heritage."

Understanding blazed through Kara's mind as her hands moved. Where her energy met Zayn's, new realities blossomed—tiny pocket dimensions that held worlds of possibility. She saw how they could create safe havens, healing spaces, bridges between realms that Project Chimera could never touch.

"This is incredible," Zayn whispered, watching as their combined power spawned miniature galaxies between them. "We're not just protecting reality…"

"We're helping it grow," Shukára finished, awe in her voice, "evolve, become more than it was."

Shani nodded. "Now you begin to understand. Project Chimera seeks to control reality. But you—you can nurture it, help it flourish in ways they could never imagine."

She gestured, and a door appeared in the air beside them. "Come. There is more you must know. Your brother Quin passed through here, leaving messages I was to share only when you were ready."

"Quin was here?" Kara's heart leaped.

"And learned much of what I'm about to teach you," Shani confirmed. "Though his path led him to a different revelation. One that you must discover in your own time."

As they followed her toward a crystal palace made of frozen time, Kara felt hope blazing brighter than ever. With each step, her new understandings settled into her being, adding new layers to her core.

Behind them, Marcus frantically took notes, his mind already theorizing how this creative force could counter Project Chimera. The others watched in amazement as reality seemed to sing around their footsteps.

Scene 3: The Hall of Whispers

The Hall of Whispers lived up to its name. Knowledge rippled through the air like waves of heat on a summer horizon, taking form as shimmering texts before dissolving back into pure thought. The crystalline walls held memories like frozen moments, each one waiting to be awakened.

Shani led them to the center of the vast chamber, where a pool of liquid starlight rippled with untold secrets. "Place your pendants over the pool," she instructed Kara. "Let them connect with the memories stored here."

As Kara held her pendants over the surface, the liquid light shifted. Images formed: Quin standing in this spot, studying with celestial scholars. His face concentrating as he pored over texts that existed in multiple dimensions at once.

"He learned quickly," Shani said. "Perhaps too quickly. What he discovered here led him to investigate Project Chimera more deeply."

The pool's surface changed, showing Project Chimera's true plan unfolding like a dark flower. They did not infect randomly—but in a pattern that stretched across dimensions, all pointing toward a single goal.

"The Heart of Worlds," Kara breathed. "They're not just trying to control it. They're trying to—"

"Rewrite it," Zayn finished, his storm energy crackling with concern. "Change its fundamental nature."

Marcus stepped closer, his tablet recording everything. "These patterns... they're creating a network of veilrot, like a virus, that could alter the basic laws of reality."

A new image formed in the pool—Quin making a discovery that caused him to step back in shock. But before they could see what he'd found, the memory faded.

"Some truths can only be understood and fully appreciated when discovered firsthand," Shani said. "Your brother knew this. That's why he left clues rather than answers."

"Can you at least tell us where he went?" Kara asked.

Shani's eyes held ancient wisdom and subtle warning. "To understand what you seek, you must first prove yourselves worthy. The Trials of the Sky await."

The chamber shifted around them, the walls becoming transparent to reveal a series of floating platforms among the clouds. Each shimmering platform held a custom challenge.

"Your unique abilities will be tested," Shani explained. "Not just your powers, but your understanding of when to use them—and when to refrain."

Kara and Zayn exchanged determined looks. Haven prepared for war. Somewhere Quin waited with crucial knowledge, and the hidden Heart of Worlds lay on the brink of attack. Everything depended on them passing these trials.

"We're ready," Kara declared, her pendants pulsing with purpose.

Above them, the paths between platforms glowed like bridges made of starlight, waiting to be crossed.

Scene 4: Trials of the Sky

The first platform hovered in the endless expanse of the Ethereal City's skyscape, a crystalline surface that seemed to float on light. As Kara stepped onto it, the trial began. The surrounding air filled with illusions of her deepest fears—Project Chimera's veilrot reaching The Heart of Worlds, reality fracturing under their control, Haven falling to darkness.

"Face your fears," Shani's voice echoed, "but do not let them control you."

Kara's pendants blazed as the illusions pressed closer. Her instinct said to fight, to unleash her full Guardian strength against these shadows. But something in Shani's words made her pause.

"It's not about fighting," she realized. "It's about understanding."

She closed her eyes, letting her fear wash over her without resistance. As she accepted each fear, acknowledged its presence without letting it control her, the illusions transformed. Each shadow revealed a deeper truth about the impact of choice, of standing firm even in darkness.

Zayn, Marcus, Noni, Keairra, and Caid each faced their own trials, each platform revealing crucial lessons about the nature of power and responsibility. As they progressed, their challenges interweaved, requiring them to work together in complex ways.

The final platform brought them all together. Here, they faced a miniature version of their ultimate challenge—The Heart of Worlds under siege. And like their actual mission, conventional means would end in defeat.

"The Heart must be protected," Shani reminded them, "but not through force alone."

Kara looked at her companions, each of them bringing unique insights from their individual trials. Together, they worked not to defeat the illusionary threat, but to strengthen The Heart through understanding and balance.

As they completed the last trial, the platforms merged into a single crystalline surface. Shani descended to meet them, approval shining in her celestial eyes.

"You've proven yourselves worthy," she declared. "Not because you're powerful, but because you understand the true nature of guardianship. The Heart of Worlds doesn't need warriors—it needs protectors who understand that power is nothing without wisdom."

Shani raised her hands, and stardust gathered between her palms, coalescing into a device unlike anything they'd seen. It resembled a compass, but its needle responded to currents of reality rather than magnetic fields. Constellations danced across its crystal face, and its edges shifted through spectrums of light that had no names.

"The Celestial Compass," she said, presenting it to Kara. "It will guide you through the realms that lie between here and The Heart of Worlds. But remember—it points to where you need to go, not always where you want to go."

As Kara took the compass, her pendants resonated with it. The device came alive in her hands, its face showing their next destination—a realm where ancient forests grew through the fabric of time.

"The Enchanted Forest," Shani nodded. "Where nature and magic are one. What you learn there will be crucial for protecting The Heart."

The compass pulsed with gentle light, already aligning itself with the energy that would guide their journey.

"Thank you," Kara said, understanding the value of this gift. The compass would be essential in navigating the complex paths ahead, leading them to truth, leading them to The Heart of Worlds.

Scene 5: The Enchanted Forest

The Celestial Compass guided them through a portal of twisting light, leading to a forest where trees grew as tall as mountains. Sunlight filtered through canopies that existed in multiple seasons at once—branches bore spring blossoms, summer leaves, autumn colors, and winter frost.

Kara sensed the disturbance before they saw it. A sickness crept through parts of the forest, turning vibrant growth dull and lifeless. Her pendants pulsed with concern, detecting the subtle wrongness that threaded through the natural magic.

"Something's wrong with the forest's heart," Zayn murmured, his storm energy picking up discordant notes in the woodland's song.

A fae emerged from between the trees—Aelin, her wings shimmering like dewdrops in the morning light. Despite her ethereal beauty, worry etched lines across her brow. She startled at the sight of them, unprepared for visitors in these troubled times.

"You're not shadowbound," she said with surprise, studying them. "We've had to turn away so many travelers, fear of the blight..."

"What is this blight?" Kara already moving toward an affected area. The forest's pain called to her Guardian senses.

"It started in the ancient grove," Aelin explained. "At first we thought it natural, but it spreads wrong. Heals wrong. Even our strongest magic can't—"

Kara didn't hesitate. "Show us."

Aelin led them to a grove where ancient trees wept sap that glowed with sickly light. The forest's song turned discordant here, natural harmonies twisted into painful rhythms.

The team moved into action. Kara and Zayn combined their essence, weaving harmonies that called to the forest's true nature. Marcus analyzed the blight's patterns while Noni and Keairra contained its spread. Caid's elemental abilities helped restore balance to the affected areas.

Hours passed as they worked to ease the forest's pain. Gradually, the sickness retreated. Trees straightened, their songs returning to pure notes. Life flowed back into damaged areas, stronger for having overcome the blight.

Aelin watched in amazement as health returned to her forest. "You did this freely, without asking anything in return."

"The forest needed healing," Kara replied. "That was enough."

The fae's expression shifted from gratitude to determination. "Let me guide you through our realm. The forest has many secrets, and the path ahead holds dangers. It's the least I can do for all you have done for our land," she added, seeing their hesitation. "It is what's right."

The Celestial Compass hummed in agreement, its needle aligning with Aelin's path. Their destination lay ahead, but they had gained something precious—trust given, born from kindness offered.

Scene 6: The Riddle of the Ancients

Deep in the Enchanted Forest, where time flowed like sap through ancient bark, they found the standing stones. Each monolith bore symbols identical to those Kara had seen in the Ethereal City, but these pulsed with earth magic rather than celestial power.

"The Circle of Seasons," Aelin breathed. "None have decoded its patterns since the First Age."

The stones formed a perfect circle, but their arrangement felt wrong, discordant. Kara's pendants resonated with them, suggesting a different configuration. The Celestial Compass spun in her hand, its face showing overlapping patterns of energy.

"Look," she pointed to recurring symbols. "They match the harmonic patterns we used in the Ethereal City, but they're... inverted?"

"Not inverted," Zayn moving to study another stone. "Grounded. Flowing from highest energy."

Marcus recorded the patterns while Noni and Keairra traced the energy flows between stones. Caid placed his hand on the central stone, feeling the elemental pulse.

Understanding bloomed in Kara's mind. "It's a lock," she said. "But also a key. The stones don't just need to be aligned—they need to sing together."

Working together, they shifted the massive stones. Each movement precise, guided by the compass and the resonance of Kara's pendants. As each stone found its true place, it hummed with deep earthen tones.

The last stone clicked into position. The circle erupted with green-gold light, pure. A wave of healing energy burst outward, racing through the forest like sunlight breaking through storm clouds. Where it passed, the trees grew stronger, their natural defenses enhanced against any future illness.

But the stones continued. Their combined song formed images in the air—showing their next destination, a lake that reflected more than mere physical reality.

"The Mirror Lake," Aelin gasped. "Where truth cannot hide from itself."

The compass aligned with this new direction, but also revealed something more. The stone circle had become a permanent anchor of protection, now woven into the forest's own defenses. Any future attempt to veilrot this realm would face not just the forest's natural resistance, but the combined force of earth and celestial magic defending in harmony.

"You've done more than solve a riddle," Aelin said. "You've awakened ancient protections we'd forgotten existed."

The forest sang around them, its voice stronger and clearer than before. Tomorrow they would head to the Mirror Lake, but tonight they had given this realm back a piece of its ancient strength.

Scene 7: The Mirror Lake

The Mirror Lake stretched before them like liquid starlight, its surface still despite the forest breeze. As they approached, their reflections showed not their physical forms, but manifestations of their pure potential.

"The lake shows what lies dormant within," Aelin explained. "Powers waiting to awaken."

Kara and Zayn stood at the lake's edge, their reflections merging. Where the images overlapped, a new form of energy sparked—neither his storm power nor her harmonics, but something different.

"Join hands," Aelin's eyes sparked with recognition. "The lake reveals a Guardian art not seen since the First Age."

As their hands clasped, their pendants pulsed in perfect sync. The Aether surged between them, and as they stood side by side—their energies interwove at a quantum level.

The merge hit like lightning meeting thunder. Shy felt Zayn's storm energy crash into her light, felt their spirits spiral together into something new, something magnificent, penetrating her essence.

Speed coursed through them like wildfire. Strength sang in their merged form. "This is..." she began through their shared consciousness. His wonder echoed through her. "I know."

"The Phoenix Merge," Aelin whispered in awe.

Their combined form blazed with light. Kara's harmonious ability to manipulate reality merged with Zayn's storm essence, created a form that crackled with pure energy. Wings of lightning spread from their joined power, and where they touched the ground, reality rippled.

"This is incredible," Kara gasped, feeling how they amplified each other. Every movement they made together sent waves of purifying energy through multiple dimensions at once. When they moved in sync, they could generate bursts of immense energy that felt pure.

Marcus's tablet sparked from trying to record the energy levels.

Kara and Zayn tested the Phoenix Merge, discovering they could move with the speed of lightning, generate shields of pure energy, and unleash waves of pure amplified Aether.

"The Phoenix Merge was meant for these times," Aelin explained. "When darkness threatens reality, two Guardians can unite their essence to become a force of renewal."

Their reflections in the lake showed the possibilities—possibilities that could develop as their bond grew stronger. But it also showed the responsibility such great power carried. Used wrongly, even for a moment, such force could cause as much damage as the veilrot they race against.

As they separated, both Kara and Zayn knew they had gained more than just a new ability. They had discovered a deeper level of trust and connection that would be crucial in the path ahead.

The Celestial Compass hummed, its face showing their next adventure, The Time Weaver. And now they had a new shared ability—one that could turn the tide when they confronted Project Chimera's forces.

Scene 8: The Time Weaver

The path from the Mirror Lake led them to a grove where time seemed to pool like morning mist. At its center stood the Time Weaver, her form shifting between young and old, past and future. Threads of possibility flowed through her fingers like living light.

"I have seen your arrivals a thousand times," her voice echoing through multiple moments at once. "And your questions remain the same—how to protect The Heart without destroying all that Project Chimera has bound."

The Time Weaver gestured, and reality rippled around them. Different futures played out like parallel streams: worlds where veilrot dominated, worlds where the fight against it destroyed as much as it saved, and threads of possibility that achieved balance—some at great costs.

"The Phoenix Merge you've discovered," she nodded to Kara and Zayn, "it features in the futures where hope survives. Its ability to separate corruption from the corrupted... this is key."

She reached into the flows of time and pulled forth an hourglass that sparkled with temporal energy. Sand from crushed stars flowed between its chambers, creating colorful, intricate patterns.

"This will help you combat those who twist time to their advantage," she explained. "Project Chimera has learned to manipulate temporal flows. This will protect you from their attempts to trap you in distorted time."

The Time Weaver's form tensed, her eyes seeing something distant and troubling. "Time is of the essence now," she announced. "The Realm of the Forgotten awaits." With that, she faded into the temporal mists, leaving them with the hourglass and a sense of growing urgency.

Scene 9: Realm of the Forgotten

Mist curled around their feet as they entered the Realm of the Forgotten, a place where lost memories and abandoned dreams drifted like shadows. Echoes of countless stories whispered through the air, each one a fragment of something—or someone—left behind.

Here, Project Chimera's true plan revealed itself through scattered pieces of intelligence. Fragments of conversations, glimpses of secret meetings, and traces of experiments too horrible to comprehend swirled through the mists.

"They're not just trying to control The Heart," Kara said, her pendants cutting through the obscuring fog. "They're trying to use it to rewrite the rules of reality. To make veilrot the dominant state of existence."

Through the swirling mists, they saw visions of Project Chimera's facilities across multiple realms, all working toward this single devastating goal. They did not corrupt at random—but targeted boundaries for something much worse to come.

The hourglass pulsed with warning as temporal distortions rippled through the realm. They edged closer to the truth, as Project Chimera raced them to the Heart of Worlds.

The mists of the Forgotten Realm parted to reveal an ancient archway covered in symbols that pulsed with primordial mystique. The Celestial Compass spun violently before pointing straight up, its face showing overlapping patterns of all the realms they'd visited.

"This is it," Kara yelled over the new whirling energy in the room, holding the Time Weaver's hourglass. "The gateway to The Heart!"

The hourglass resonated with the archway's symbols, its star-sand flowing in improbable patterns. As Kara held it up, time and space twisted around them, a deafening roar filling the air.

"The hourglass isn't just for protection," Marcus shouted, watching reality fold. "It seems to be a key."

Zayn's storm energy synchronized with the temporal flows. "One that works for those who've proven worthy through all the trials."

The archway awakened, its symbols blazing with light. But instead of opening a simple portal, it deconstructed reality around them layer by layer. They felt themselves being drawn upward, passing through every realm as they ascended to the one place that connected them all.

When the light faded, they stood in the sanctuary of The Heart of Worlds, the birthplace of reality.

Scene 10: The Guardian of The Heart

The sanctuary of The Heart of Worlds defied description. Reality seemed to originate from this point, flowing outward like rivers of pure creation. The air shimmered with raw potential, each breath containing the essence of a thousand worlds.

Before them stood The Heart's Guardian, a being of pure light and purpose. Their form shifted between all shapes, as if no single form could contain their true nature.

"To reach this place," the Guardian's voice resonated through their beings, "you have passed through many trials. But the ultimate test lies in what you would give up to protect all that is."

The Guardian gestured, and before each of them appeared a manifestation of what they held most dear. For Marcus, his accumulated knowledge. For Noni, her connection to magic. For Keairra and Caid, their elemental bonds.

In front of Kara appeared her last physical connection to her past and to Quin—the pendant she'd worn since birth. The thought of surrendering this connection to Quin and to many of her new found abilities made her heart ache.

"To protect The Heart," the Guardian explained, "you must be willing to sacrifice your own."

Without hesitation, Kara removed her original pendant. The moment she surrendered it, something changed. Power flooded through her remaining pendant—not of loss, but of transcendence. The Guardian nodded, understanding flowing between them.

"You give up not for personal gain, but for the good of all realms," they said. "This makes you worthy." The Guardian's form solidified. "The Heart has chosen you, Shukára Vallian. In times of greatest need, you too will serve as its protector."

Before anyone could respond, the ground beneath them shook. Project Chimera had found them.

Scene 11: Confrontation with Project Chimera

Reality rippled as Project Chimera's forces breached the sanctuary's outer barriers. Captain Reed led the assault, her voidtouched form now almost unrecognizable, trailing streams of sickly green energy that corroded everything it touched.

"The Heart of Worlds," Reed's distorted voice echoed. "All that power... just waiting to be harnessed." Her gaze fixed on Kara. "One last chance. Join us in reshaping reality."

"You still don't understand," Kara's remaining pendant blazing with pure light. "The Heart isn't meant to be controlled. It's meant to be protected."

Reed laughed, the sound fracturing the space around her. "Then we'll take it by force."

The battle erupted across multiple layers of reality. Shadowbound soldiers phased through dimensional barriers while modified portal devices tried to tear holes in the sanctuary's defenses. The Guardian moved to protect The Heart, creating shields of pure light.

"Now!" Kara called to Zayn. Their hands clasped, and the Phoenix Merge manifested in a burst of purifying light. Moving with lightning speed, they crashed through the enemy lines, their Aether waves striking veilrot without harming the beings trapped within it.

Marcus disrupted their portal devices, while Noni and the others defended the sanctuary's key points. The Time Weaver's hourglass protected them from temporal attacks, its tethers keeping them anchored in normal time.

But Reed had one last weapon. She activated something in her armor, and reality screamed. A modified portal formed around The Heart, trying to infect its pure essence.

"If we can't control it," Reed snarled, "we will poison it!"

The Guardian's light strained against the assault. "The Heart must not fall!"

Through the Phoenix Merge, Kara and Zayn could see the truth—Reed trying to harm The Heart, and trying to change its nature. If she succeeded, corruption would become the natural state of reality.

Racing against time, they launched a desperate counterattack. The battle reached its crescendo as pure power met veilrot in a clash that shook the foundations of reality.

Still merged, Kara and Zayn unleashed an attack on Reed's portal device. Their lightning speed let them dance between waves of corruption while their shields deflected the worst of her attacks. But even with their combined strength, the device continued its work, its toxic energy reaching for The Heart.

"You can't stop progress," Reed laughed, though her voice held an edge of madness. "Evolution demands sacrifice!"

Kara understood. Through the Phoenix Merge, she could see the currents flowing through everything—including through Reed. The captain channeled something darker, something ancient, that pulled her strings.

"Zayn," she communicated through their merged consciousness, "the device isn't the target."

In perfect sync, they changed tactics. Instead of attacking the portal device, they focused their Aether waves on Reed. The force of their combined essence struck the veilrot, but this time with surgical precision, targeting the foreign influence that had taken root in her.

Reed screamed as the malevolent force tore away from her essence. The portal device, cut off from its source, destabilized. Reality trembled as Reed fell to her knees, her form flickering between corrupted and original states.

"What... what have you done?" she gasped.

The Phoenix Merge let them maintain their assault while Kara spoke. "Showed you the difference between evolution and corruption. Between progress and destruction."

With a final wave, they severed Reed's connection to the dark force controlling her. She collapsed under her own control again but fell into unconsciousness, while her forces fell into disarray. The portal device imploded, taking its veilrot with it.

But even as they celebrated this victory, Kara sensed something dark retreating into the spaces between realities. Ancient and patient, the force controlling Reed remained undefeated, merely set back in this round.

Reed stirred, her eyes clear for the first time in months. "I remember everything," she whispered, horror creeping into her voice. "Who I chose to partner with...What they made me do..."

"Then help us stop them," Kara offered, the Phoenix Merge dissolving as she and Zayn separated. "Tell us everything you know."

Reed's core beliefs hadn't shifted. "Kara, we must control The Heart to save humanity."

Kara looked around at the destruction. "How many have you lost trying to save humanity?"

"Fewer than we'd lose doing nothing!" But doubt crept into Reed's eyes. "The power had to be controlled. Had to be... to be..."

Reed's eyes widened in terror. "No," she whispered.

A portal of pure darkness ripped open beneath her. Shadowy tendrils, far more ancient and terrible than Project Chimera's, wrapped around Reed's form. Her scream cut off. The dark forces yanked her into the void, leaving her echo behind: "Noooooooooo!"

The portal snapped shut with a sound like reality shattering, leaving them with the chilling realization that the true enemy held far more power than they'd imagined.

Scene 12: Protecting The Heart

The Guardian of The Heart approached as the last echoes of battle faded. "You see now," they said, "why The Heart must be protected differently. Our old ways of guardianship are not enough against what comes."

Kara studied The Heart of Worlds, its pure energy flowing out to all realms. An idea formed—not of walls or weapons, but of connection.

"What if we linked The Heart to all realms?" she suggested. "Not to control it, but to share its protection. Let every realm have a stake in its safety."

The Guardian's form shifted with interest. "To distribute among the Guardians of each realm... it has never been attempted."

"Because it would limit any one being's control," Zayn realized. "Including ours."

"Exactly," Kara nodded. "No single entity could corrupt or control it. We'd all be responsible for its protection."

Marcus added. "Decentralized security is the highest form of security."

The Guardian considered the proposal, their form shifting through countless possibilities. "Such an action would fundamentally change how The Heart interacts with reality. It would be... shared, and more resilient."

Kara placed her hand near The Heart's energy. "Better to share pure power and lessen the risk of it being corrupted. Every realm would become its guardian."

"The responsibility would be enormous," the Guardian warned. "Each realm would need to understand their role, learn to work together in ways they never have before."

"They already are," Kara smiled, thinking of Haven's united forces. "We've seen it happening. They just need a reason to make it permanent."

With the Guardian's guidance, they began a linking ritual. Kara channeled The Heart's power through her pendant, while Zayn helped stabilize the flows. Marcus recorded the process while Noni, Keairra, and Caid represented the different magical disciplines that would need to work in harmony.

The Heart's power flowed outward in new patterns, seeking worthy guardians in each realm. Where it touched, it left small nexus points—not enough power to corrupt or control, but enough to create a network of protection.

As the ritual completed, they felt the change ripple through reality. The Heart reinforced, no longer exposed to a single point of attack. Now positioned at the center of a vast web of connected guardians, each responsible for their own realm's connection to the whole.

As the connections established themselves, The Heart pulsed with renewed vigor. It had become something more resilient, more powerful—a shared source of strength only accessed through cooperation and harmony.

"It's done," the Guardian announced, their form now more stable, as if The Heart's new configuration had settled their own essence. "From this moment, The Heart's protection depends not on walls or weapons, but on the unity of realms."

Kara felt the change in her pendant—it now hummed stronger through interconnection. Each realm's new guardian would feel this same connection, this same responsibility.

"The ancient evil will not give up easily," the Guardian warned. "Already their forces move against multiple realms, seeking to break this new alliance."

Scene 13: Returning to Haven

Haven's central plaza erupted in celebration as they returned through a portal of pure light. The united forces had held against Project Chimera's armies, and now they felt the additional strength of their connection to The Heart.

Thorne's massive form emerged from the shadows, his expression grave. "The battle is far from over," he paused. "The dark forces have not relinquished their plans."

Kara nodded, remembering the ancient shadows that had dragged Reed away. "They've been spreading fear and false information across the realms for years. Building their forces."

"And now they'll be desperate," Thorne agreed. "Now that we have had a victory, they will try anything to steal it from us. You've given us a fighting chance," he rumbled. "But the enemy sends forces against every realm that joined The Heart's protection. They mean to break us. They will come with both the shadowbound and those who chose corruption willingly, the voidtouched."

Kara squeezed Zayn's hand, drawing strength from their connection. "Then we'll teach them what unity really means."

Around them, Haven pulsed with determination as warriors from countless realms prepared to aid their new allies. The war had not ended—it had entered its final phase. But now, for the first time, all realms faced it together.

CHAPTER 7: ANCIENT FORCES

Scene 1: The Arrival of Allies

Haven's warning bells rang across multiple realms as the first distress calls arrived. Northern realms under siege. Desert temples falling. Forest kingdoms burning. But with each dire report came an answer that shook reality—the arrival of allies ready for war.

Elven warships burst through aurora-lit portals, their crystal hulls already crackling with battle magic. They paused long enough for their captains to salute Haven's towers before racing toward the embattled Northern Kingdoms, war-songs echoing across dimensions.

"Forest kingdoms report heavy casualties!" a Wind Rider shouted, her wings scorched from flying through combat zones.

As if in answer, the skies split with a thunder that shook Haven's foundations. The Dragon Riders of the Crimson Realm emerged, some still bearing marks of recent battles. Their mounts' scales gleamed like fresh blood in Haven's many suns, their battle-roars defying the veilrot.

"Fight's already started without us," their leader grinned, dragon flame reflecting in her eyes. "Can't have that."

The central plaza transformed into a staging ground, where ancient opponents now stood shoulder to shoulder. Dwarven War-Masters raised their runic hammers alongside

Elven Spellsingers. Frost Giants helped Fire Lords position their siege engines. Each group added their power to Haven's defenses even as they prepared for immediate deployment.

Through it all, moments of pure majesty had pierced the urgency of war. The Dragon Rider squadron had soared in perfect formation over Haven's spires, their mounts breathing streams of flame that transformed into signals of alliance. Elven ships had performed a traditional honor-pass, their crystal hulls singing with light. Even the Dwarven battle-platforms, the practical warriors, had arrived with their ancient runes blazing in patterns unseen since the First Age.

Surrounded by their war maps, Kara coordinated with commanders from a dozen realms while Zayn organized strike teams. Multiple fronts would require the Phoenix Merge.

"The Desert Temples can't hold much longer." Marcus's enhanced tablet tracked battles across realities. "They could use the Phoenix Merge!"

"Dragon Riders can reach them fastest," Kara decided. "Support from Wind Mages for tactical strikes. And the Phoenix Merge will not be far behind!"

"Northern Kingdoms need more support," a Dwarven commander added. "Our platforms are ready, but the approach is heavily defended."

"Then we give them something they've never seen before," Zayn stepped forward. "Dwarven platforms carried through Elven star-portals, protected by Dragon fire."

The commanders exchanged fierce grins. Project Chimera had never seen unified realms before. But today, the unified realms would give them a demonstration.

A last group of allies emerged from a portal of pure brightness—the Celestial Warriors of the Ethereal City, their armor forged from condensed starlight. They arrived in formation, each carrying a banner that shimmered with constellation patterns.

"Haven stands with all realms," Kara declared to the assembled forces. "Today we fight... we fight as one!"

The roar of approval shook reality. Dragon calls merged with Elven war-songs, Dwarven battle-cries harmonized with Wind Mage chants. The air crackled with combined power as the first strike teams prepared to deploy.

Scene 2: Desert Storm Rising

Desert Temples of the Desert Realm pierced the sky like ancient spears, their golden spires catching light from three suns. Sacred runes blazed along their surfaces, holding back vile waves that pulsed with green light. Temple Guardians, their robes shimmering with protective magic, fought with desperate grace to protect their ancient halls.

Then came the sound that turned the tide—the harmonic roar of dragons in formation. The Crimson Wing burst through a reality-fold, fifty dragons strong, their scales blazing like fresh flame in the triple sunlight. Leader Sara FireHeart, standing on her dragon's back, her battle-robes trailing fire as she conducted her squadron like a symphony.

"Wind Mages!" she called, her voice carrying on magic-touched air. "Show us your dance!"

The Wind Dancers of the Cloud Spires responded, their silver robes catching updrafts as they wove through the air. They moved like living mercury, creating spiraling corridors of pure air magic that the dragons could ride. Where wind met dragon-flame, new magic bloomed.

Zayn watched from a high temple spire, storm energy crackling around him. "Ready?" he asked Kara, his eyes beginning to shift from human to that otherworldly silver-blue.

"Always," she smiled, taking his hand.

As the Phoenix Merge began, Zayn let his true nature emerge. Storm clouds gathered fast in the desert sky, and his wolf aspect manifested around their merged form, a giant beast of lightning and storm—The Blue Wolf—running on air. Their combined power sent waves of purifying energy across the battlefield while the wolf's howl shook reality.

Dragon Riders cheered at the sight, their mounts breathing fresh flame in salute. The Blue Wolf leaped between reality layers, storms trailing in their wake, while dragons dove through the lightning-charged air to strike at evil with renewed purpose.

Sara directed her forces with fluid grace, each gesture bringing new combinations of power. "Weave with us!" she called to the merged Guardians. Dragons began flying in patterns around The Blue Wolf, their flames joining Zayn's storms to create a tempest of cleansing fire.

Below, Temple Guardians found their ancient magic responding to the combined forces above. Sacred runes blazed brighter, synchronized with dragon flame and storm. The temples seemed to sing, their spires resonating with the pure joy of forces united.

Wind Mages danced through it all, their silver robes now streaming with rainbow light as they conducted the air into songs of power. They created bridges of solid wind between temples, roads of light that dragons could charge along, their flames leaving trails of purifying magic.

Project Chimera's forces had faced nothing like this unity. Their corruption-tech sparked and failed against magic wielded with such natural harmony. The Blue Wolf's howl shattered their dimensional anchors while dragon flame burned away their vile bonds.

The beauty of it all struck the deepest blow against evil—the magnificent dance of dragons against triple suns, Wind Mages weaving silver light between golden spires, and at the heart of it all, a wolf made of storm, running through reality, trailing lightning and hope.

Victory rose like dawn across the desert as the last veilrot burned away. Dragons roared in triumph, their voices joining the wolf's song. The Desert Temples blazed with renewed intensity, their ancient magic awakened and strengthened by the unity of realms.

Sara landed her dragon near the merged Guardians. As they separated, Zayn and Kara faded back into human form. Their eyes shone with fierce joy. Kara, having felt the wolf's passion as part of the merge, howled to the sky, causing Zayn and then Kara herself to burst into laughter.

Kara looked at Zayn. "Let's do that again!"

"Now that," Sara grinned, "is how realms fight together."

Around them, Wind Mages began a victory dance, their magic painting auroras across the desert sky. Dragons launched into the air in perfect formation, breathing streams of flame that wrote ancient runes of protection above the temples.

The Desert Temples didn't just survive—they transformed, renewed by the unity that saved them. And in that moment, every warrior there understood: this marked the beginning of what their combined strength could achieve.

Scene 3: Shadows Rising

Back at Haven to coordinate their next strikes, Kara and Zayn witnessed the command post hum with victory reports. Crystalline displays showed battles turning across multiple realms—Dwarven platforms breaking sieges in the North, Elven ships rescuing coastal kingdoms, armies uniting with unprecedented success.

A Wind Rider burst through the dimensional doors, her silver uniform scorched, eyes wide. "Commander!" She stumbled forward, catching herself on the strategic table. "The Shadow Peaks... we saw... they moved like smoke but struck like thunder."

"Breathe, Rider," Kara steadied her. "What did you see?"

"Two figures, dark as void. They... they merged, like your Phoenix Merge, but wrong. The mountains seemed to recoil. Half our squadron... gone. Not killed, erased, like they never existed." Her hands shook. "They're coming... They said Haven's next."

The chamber's light crystals dimmed, shadows deepening in the corners. Temperature dropped as reality seemed to thin.

"Not next." Storm energy crackling around Zayn. "Now!"

Through the chamber's windows, two figures descended from Haven's highest spires, moving like liquid darkness, their grace unnatural. As they touched down, their presence thickened the air with shadow.

The Shadow Duo. Former Guardians, their form twisted into something terrible. Where Phoenix Merge brought harmony, their dark fusion created discord that hurt the eyes to witness.

"Haven," one spoke, voice echoing. "Last bastion of the old ways."

"Time to embrace the new," the other finished, shadows writhing around them both.

Kara and Zayn moved to the chamber's center as others backed away. This fight wouldn't be like the Desert Temples. This fight would herald power versus power and light against dark, with Haven's heart at stake.

Scene 4: The Light Dims

The chamber erupted into chaos as the Shadow Duo launched their first attack. Kara and Zayn merged, their Phoenix form blazing with light against the encroaching darkness. They moved with lightning speed, striking at the foul pair from multiple angles.

But the Shadow Duo matched them move for move, their dark form flowing like liquid night. Where Phoenix speed met shadow speed, reality crackled with the impact. The battles across Haven's spires became a blur of light against dark, neither able to gain advantage.

"You can't outrace your own shadow," the Duo taunted in voices of harmonic dissonance.

The Phoenix Merge shifted tactics, engaging in direct combat. Power met power as they clashed above Haven's crystal towers. Each impact sent shockwaves through multiple dimensions, shattering windows and cracking stone. Yet again, they matched each other—every strike countered, every strategy mirrored.

"Time to end this," Kara communicated through the merge. Their form blazed brighter as they summoned their cleansing wave, the power that had freed so many from Project Chimera's control.

The purifying energy washed over the Shadow Duo... and did nothing. Their dark form laughed, the sound distorting reality around them.

"Fool's light," they mocked. "We chose this. There's nothing to cleanse when darkness is embraced."

The Shadow Duo countered with their own wave of pure darkness, forcing the Phoenix Merge back. For the first time, fear crept in. Their three greatest advantages—speed, combat, and cleansing—had failed.

"All that light," the Duo's voice rippled with malice, "and still so blind to true power."

Haven's defenders watched in growing dread as their champions, for the first time, seemed to be outmatched.

Scene 5: Wolf Phoenix

Power flowed into the Phoenix Merge from every corner of Haven. Dragon fire spiraled up the crystal spires, Wind Mage silver streamed through the air, Dwarven runes blazed from the foundations. Each ally's strength added to their light, not just lending power, but creating something new. With the energy from the allies, they summoned a new level of being. A brighter and more formidable presence manifested. The nascent Wolf Phoenix drew gasps from the arena. Both natures presenting at once was unprecedented. The combined essence of Kara and Zayn brought forth something never seen before.

The Shadow Duo struck again, but this time, their darkness shattered against a shield woven from multiple magics. They attacked from another angle, only to be driven back by a wave of combined Dragon flame and Wind Mage power, guided by the Wolf Phoenix's light.

"Impossible," the Duo snarled, their dark form rippling with uncertainty.

"No," the Wolf Phoenix responded, rising into Haven's sky. "This is what you never understood. Real power isn't about domination."

Light erupted from every crystal in Haven, every spire and tower pulsing in harmony. The Wolf Phoenix became a nexus of pure radiance, each ally's power adding its own color to their aura. Dragons circled them in perfect formation, their flames creating a spiral of energy. Wind Mages danced through the air, their silver magic weaving patterns of force.

The Shadow Duo launched themselves upward in desperate attack, their darkness boiling against the night sky. But they no longer faced just two Guardians. They slammed into a wall of unified power—Dwarven runes blazing beneath their feet, Elven spells singing through the air, natural magic rising from Haven's foundations.

For the first time, fear crept into the Duo's dissonant voice. They tried to retreat, but powers they'd mocked trapped them in a sphere of combined magic.

The Wolf Phoenix raised their hands, conducting this symphony of unified strength. "Let us show you what power really means."

Haven seemed to inhale—every crystal, every ally, every current drawing in at once—before releasing a pulse of pure, unified energy that illuminated reality. The wave carried the essence of life.

The Shadow Duo's dark form couldn't maintain cohesion against such force. Their corruption blew away like smoke in a storm, leaving them separated and stripped of their twisted abilities.

As the light faded, Haven's defenders cheered. Dragons roared in triumph, Wind Mages painted victory in silver across the sky, and the crystal spires sang anew. The Shadow Duo lay unconscious and purified, their darkness replaced by possibility.

The Wolf Phoenix separated, Kara and Zayn standing, hearts still racing after feeling the full essence of each other, Kara feeling Zayn's wolfen embrace and Zayn feeling her full aetheric winged caress. But something had changed. Haven's transformation had left its mark on them, showing them a glimpse of what true unity could achieve.

"That..." Zayn said, looking at their unconscious combatants, "that hurts."

Kara nodded, watching allies gather the former Shadow Duo. "Once, they were like us—until they lost their way, misled by falsehoods, seduced by fear, and fed the fires of division. Redemption belongs to all who seek it."

Above them, Haven's many suns broke through the clouds, painting the crystal spires in colors of hope. They had faced their dark reflection and discovered something greater than mere might—they discovered the true strength of unity.

Scene 6: Giants

Haven's central spire blazed as Kara and Zayn, in Phoenix Merge form, reinforced dimensional barriers. The Shadow Duo's attack had compromised several of Haven's defensive layers. With battles still raging across multiple realms, they couldn't risk their central fortress falling.

"Northern quadrant stabilized," Marcus called from his monitoring station. "But the eastern barriers are still fluctuating."

Through their merged consciousness, Kara and Zayn directed pure energy into Haven's crystal matrix. Each repaired connection had to be perfect—one weak point could endanger everything they'd built. Dragon Riders patrolled the dimensional gaps while they worked, ensuring no enemies slipped through.

The first reports of The Colossus came as whispers. A mountain moving in the Outer Realms. Tremors that felt like footsteps. Villages evacuated.

"Probably earth elementals," someone in the war room said, studying sketchy images. "Though the locals seem pretty spooked."

More reports arrived. A forest laid flat in seconds. A lake drunk dry. Each account came bigger than the last, but with the Phoenix Merge occupied maintaining Haven's defenses, and battles requiring immediate attention across six different realms, who could investigate mere rumors?

Thorne studied the pattern of destruction. "I'll handle it," he rumbled, already turning to leave. "The Guardians must focus on Haven's barriers. This is likely nothing more than an unruly giant."

"You sure?" Marcus asked, a new report showing a mountain peak... missing. "These readings are getting strange."

"Our archives speak of it." Thorne's massive frame filled the doorway. "I have tamed unruly giants since before these realms were young. I shall return swiftly."

As he departed, no one noticed the ancient Rune Sage in the corner, her eyes wide with recognition as she studied the patterns of destruction. By the time she realized what they faced, Thorne had left.

"Oh no," she whispered. "It's not just any giant. It's The Colossus!"

Scene 7: The Colossus

The Rune Sage, Vara, clutched her staff tighter as the ground trembled. Even in Haven, even through layers of reality, they could feel it now. Not normal giant-steps, but something that made reality shudder.

A Wind Rider burst through the dimensional doors, her silver uniform caked with debris. "The Outer Peaks... they're gone. Not destroyed—gone. And Thorne..." She struggled to catch her breath. "He's engaging but... it's bad. The Colossus, it's the size of a mountain range!"

Through Marcus's vision window, a crystalline portal to track key warriors, they could see Thorne's distant form growing to giant size—impressive, terrifying even, reaching the height of Haven's tallest spire. However, the Colossus towered over him, its shadow darkening the realm.

"No," Vara whispered, ancient runes blazing on her staff. "Thorne, wait!"

Too late—the clash had begun, and even from Haven, they could see the overwhelming difference in scale. Thorne fought with all his ancient power, but The Colossus swatted him aside like a toy, its laugh rumbling through dimensions. "Thorny, you are no match."

In Haven's central spire, the Phoenix Merge paused in their barrier repair. "We have to help—" Kara started through their merged consciousness.

"The barriers aren't stable," Marcus warned. "If we stop now, we could lose Haven's entire defensive network. Three realms are channeling their evacuees through these paths right now!"

Another impact. Through the vision window, they saw Thorne slam into a mountain, the peak crumbling around him. The Colossus raised its foot, ready to end the fight.

Vara's voice cut through the chaos. "The ancient runes! I know how he can match its size, but I need time. Someone has to distract The Colossus!"

Scene 8: Thorne Rises

Dragon Riders launched before orders came, their mounts' wings catching cosmic fire as they soared toward the battle. Sara FireHeart led them, standing tall on her crimson drake.

"Buy the Sage time!" she roared. "Formation!"

Fifty dragons banked as one, spiraling around The Colossus's massive form. Their flames seemed insignificant against its bulk, but they commanded its attention. Wind

Mages joined them, weaving silver paths through the air that dragons could ride, multiplying their speed and precision.

The Colossus growled in annoyance, trying to swat them like flies. But dragons, born to dance through air, soared with elite precision. They dove between its fingers, flames scoring its ancient hide, each strike aimed at sensitive points.

Meanwhile, Vara knelt beside the battered Thorne, her staff blazing with runes not seen since the First Age.

Thorne, battered, looked at Vara. "Move away little one. It isn't safe for you here."

"Listen carefully," she commanded. "The old stories were true. When realms unite, ancient powers return. But size alone isn't enough—you must channel the strength of every realm you protect!"

The Colossus roared in fury as dragons continued their assault. A massive hand swept through the air, catching three riders. But before it could crush them, a blast of pure light forced its fingers open. Thorne stood, his eyes blazing with new understanding.

"The strength... of every realm," he rumbled, his voice deepening as power flowed into him. Vara's runes lifted from her staff, swirling around him in circles of ancient light.

Through Haven's vision window, the Phoenix Merge and their allies watched in awe as Thorne grew. Not just in size, but in power. Every realm that stood with Haven lent him strength. Fire from the Dragon Realms coursed through his veins. Elven starlight shone in his eyes. Dwarven earth-might flowed through his muscles.

The Colossus turned, noticing that its "small" opponent now rose to match its height. Thorne's new form blazed with the combined strength of allied realms, runes of pure energy swirling around him like constellations.

"Now then," Thorne's voice shook mountains, "shall we try this again?"

The Colossus charged, each step creating canyons, its roar shattering dimensional barriers. Black lightning crackled around its massive form as it barreled toward Thorne at full speed.

Thorne's stance shifted, ancient runes blazing brighter. A determined intensity touched his mountainous face. "Come!"

As The Colossus reached him, the power of the ancients running through Thorne's core, Thorne struck first with power and energy stored for millennia, Thorne's fist connecting to The Colossus's massive jaw.

With one blow, Thorne hurled The Colossus into the skies. Thorne hadn't finished. Before The Colossus could hit the ground, he phased through space, reappearing above it.

His fist, wrapped in the combined power of every allied realm, crashed down in a devastating blow.

The impact sent The Colossus crashing toward the earth, but Thorne appeared below, knee rising.

The knee strike launched The Colossus back up. Thorne's hands began moving in patterns taught by Wind Mage elders, creating a vortex of wind and energy.

He caught The Colossus in the tornado and gathered power for his finishing strike. Every rune on his body blazing sun-bright.

He pulled his fist back, channeling the surrounding allies. "For The Realms!" The energy grew so intense, far away dimensions felt it. The strike began in what seemed like slow motion. "I am Lord Thorne!" The blow struck with the force of a collapsing universe. The Colossus slammed into the ground with such impact that reality rippled. When the dust settled, it lay in a crater deeper than the tallest mountains, defeated.

Dragon Riders circled overhead, their mounts breathing victory flames. Wind Mages wove silver celebrations through the air. And Thorne stood tall, power of united realms still flowing through him, guardian of all he surveyed.

Thorne maintained his colossal form, runes still pulsing with the power of united realms, as he reached down to lift the unconscious giant. Dragons circled his head like fireflies around a mountain, their victory flames painting sigils of triumph across realities.

"Show off," Sara FireHeart laughed from atop her dragon, her voice carrying on Wind Mage currents.

"The old stories," Vara called up to him, her staff still glowing, "they never mentioned the fancy moves."

Thorne's laugh rumbled through dimensions. "A warrior picks up a few tricks over a few thousand years." He turned toward Haven, The Colossus secure in his grasp. "Though I must admit, that last combination proved... inspired."

In Haven's spire, the Phoenix Merge had stabilized the barriers. Kara and Zayn separated just in time to watch Thorne's victory stride, carrying his defeated opponent with the casual ease of someone who'd just discovered their true strength.

"I am Lord Thorne!" Marcus grinned, checking readings on his tablet. "That last hit registered in twelve different dimensions!"

The runes that had empowered Thorne's growth now pulsed throughout Haven's network, strengthening connections between allied realms. What began as a desperate measure had become something more—proof they thrived by working together.

Thorne shrank back to his normal size, still massive, but something had changed. The power of united realms remained with him. Runes still flickered across his skin, and his eyes held new depths of ancient might.

"Well then," he rumbled, looking around at the celebrating forces, "shall we see what other old myths turn out to be true?"

Scene 9: Victory's Dawn

Word of The Colossus's fall spread through reality like wildfire. Project Chimera's forces broke ranks deserting the Northern Kingdom, their shadowbound machines sputtering and dying as their operators fled. Across the Desert Realms, dark portals snapped shut as enemies retreated en masse. Even the shadowrends, those shadowy beasts they'd summoned slunk back into their dimensional holes.

Haven erupted in celebration. Dragons soared in triumphant formation, their flames writing ancient victory runes across multiple skies. Wind Mages danced through the air, their silver robes trailing starlight as they performed the Dances of Glory. Dwarven war-horns bellowed from their platforms, each blast carrying the deep notes of triumph.

From crystal spire to foundation stone, Haven pulsed with joy. Elven voice-weavers began the Victory Song, a melody that not heard since the First Age. Their voices carried through realms, telling the story of unity's triumph. Dragons added their harmonic roars, Wind Mages their silver songs, until the air shimmered with music.

Sara FireHeart led her Dragon Riders in the Spiral of Victory, their mounts breathing streams of pure flame that formed a double helix around Haven's tallest towers. Below, Dwarven craftsmen began etching the day's events into runestone, while Elven loremasters wove the tale into their eternal histories.

The air thrummed with a distant rhythm—the legendary Sky Drummers of the Cloud Kingdom approaching. The sound grew stronger, each beat resonating through dimensions. Dragons and Wind Mages parted to make way as the procession appeared: one-hundred drummers marching on paths of solid light, their drums blazing with each strike. Their rhythm spoke of victory, of power—a beat that made hearts race and spirits soar. Below, crowds gathered at Haven's balconies, drawn by the approaching thunder, faces lighting up as the magnificent parade drew near. The drums spoke in patterns ancient and new, telling the story of their triumph in a language everyone could understand.

Kara stood with Zayn atop Haven's central spire, watching the celebrations unfold. Their hands found each other, the Aether humming between them.

Elder Mira approached with the newly formed Allied Realm Council, their robes shimmering with the combined power of their unified worlds. She raised her hands, commanding silence from the celebrating crowds below.

"Today we witness the emergence of a Guardian not seen since the First Age," Elder Mira's voice carried across dimensions. "In Shukára Vallian, we see the rare convergence of an Aethermancer and a Veilwalker. Her mastery of the Twilight Walk rivals the ancients, while her command of pure Aether marks her as one of the strongest Aethermancers in our documented histories."

The Council members nodded in solemn agreement as Elder Mira continued, "Together with Zayn, whose Stormweaver abilities have proven legendary, they have achieved what was thought lost in time - three sacred merges. The Phoenix Merge, the Wolf Merge, and the Wolf Phoenix Merge have produced the purest Harmony Waves ever documented, cleansing corruption with unmatched power."

"The prophecies spoke true," one of the Council members added, his voice resonating with ancient power. "When storm meets Aether, when wolf meets light, an ancient force will rise. And today, that force turned our fight."

Elder Mira's eyes shone with pride as she regarded them both. "You have awakened powers long dormant, forged bonds thought lost to time. The realms stand united because you showed the way." She bowed deeply, the entire Council following suit. "Haven honors its Guardians."

A young Fae child fluttered up to them on gossamer wings, her eyes bright with both joy and curiosity. "Lady Guardian," she asked Kara, her voice chiming like tiny bells, "when evil retreats, where does it go?"

The innocent question caught Kara off guard. Before she could answer, Vara appeared beside them, her ancient staff pulsing.

"The ancients awaken," she whispered, her eyes fixed on distant horizons, "both light and dark alike."

But for now, Haven celebrated. The unified realms had faced their first true test and emerged stronger. Dragons roared, magic soared, and joy echoed through dimensions. Whatever tomorrow might bring, today belonged to victory.

EPILOGUE: DAWN OF UNITY

Scene 1: The New Haven

Morning light cascaded through Haven's crystal spires, each beam carrying the essence of multiple suns. The city had transformed, growing more beautiful with each passing day. Where once stood military fortifications, gardens now bloomed in alluring patterns, their flowers existing in multiple realities at once.

Dragons soared between new aeries built into the highest towers, their scales catching light like living gems. Below, Wind Mage teachers led students from every realm in basic flight techniques, silver magic trails criss-crossing the air as young ones learned to dance with wind.

On the outskirts of Haven, the former Shadow Duo worked in a rehabilitation realm, connected to Haven yet purposefully secluded. Here, they supported others on their journey to reconnect with light, just as they once had. Now serving as coaches for the Garden of the Second Dawn, they guided the healing process with wisdom born of experience. The Second Dawn's space pulsed with gentle energy, its architecture designed to nurture growth and renewal. In this sanctuary, those who had once been touched by darkness found understanding and purpose, transforming their past into strength.

"The garden needs these shadows to grow," one of the Duo explained to newer arrivals, gesturing to a plant that bloomed in shade. "Just as we needed our journey to become who we are now." Their eyes, once void-black, now held depth and wisdom earned through transformation.

The Realm of The Garden of the Second Dawn operated on principles of cooperation, restoration and responsibility. Those within its bounds worked with Haven's builders, healers, and teachers—as a path to rediscovering their place in reality's great dance. Each success strengthened the bonds between realms.

Thorne observed it from a high balcony, the ancient runes now etched into his skin and pulsing. Where once he stood as a warrior alone, he now led a new generation of defenders who understood that true strength came from understanding and unity.

"The old ways change," he rumbled to a group of young trainees, "and we grow stronger for it."

Scene 2: Echoes Across Realities

The Desert Temples soared higher than ever, their golden spires wrapped in dragons' protective flights. Where Project Chimera's veilrot had once threatened their foundations, rivers of pure magic now flowed through crystalline channels. Dragon Riders and Temple Guardians trained together, their combined powers creating displays that turned the desert nights into festivals of light.

"The old barriers served their purpose," Sara FireHeart said, watching young temple acolytes learning to ride dragons. "But this... this is better." Her dragon rumbled in agreement as another successful student took to the starlit sky.

Dwarven ingenuity met Elven grace. Massive bridges of living crystal spanned dimensional gaps in the Northern Kingdoms, their surfaces etched with runes of protection and welcome. Trade flowed between realms once separated by centuries of distrust. The bridges sang with travel, their harmonics a constant reminder of unity's strength.

The Forest Realms bloomed with renewed vigor. Ancient groves, once guarded, now hosted students from every realm. Young Wind Mages learned from ancient trees, while Dwarven crafters studied the living architecture of branches and vines. Knowledge flowed like spring water, enriching all it touched.

In her study in Haven's oldest tower, Vara pored over texts not opened since the First Age. Her ancient staff cast reading light that shifted through spectrums invisible to normal eyes.

"Curious," she murmured, fingers tracing patterns in a text that existed in multiple dimensions at once. "The Confluence approaches... when all Hearts align..."

Her voice trailed off as new symbols appeared on the page, responding to her touch. The runes spoke of powers deeper than any single realm, of ancient forces stirring from long slumber. Her staff pulsed with recognition of something vast approaching.

A young apprentice appeared at her door. "Master Vara? The Council requests your wisdom regarding the new dimensional anchors and—" She stopped, noticing Vara's expression. "Is everything alright?"

Vara closed the ancient text, its pages shimming with untold secrets. "Just in deep thought. Let's go advise The Council," she smiled. "When all Hearts align..." she whispered to herself, glancing back at the ancient text.

Above them, dragons danced through aurora-lit skies while Wind Mages wove paths of silver light between realms. Haven's many suns painted reality in colors of hope, even as ancient forces stirred in the depths.

Scene 3: Twin Light

Kara stood in her quarters as the sunset painted Haven's crystal spires in perfect colors. Her pendant pulsed with familiar warmth—a frequency she'd know anywhere—Quin.

The air before her shimmered, revealing him—not physically present, yet real. His image rippled like light through water, his smile remained unchanged. His pendant blazed with purpose.

"About time you got The Heart sorted," he grinned, his voice carrying echoes of distant realms.

"Quin!" Relief and joy mingled in her voice. "Where are you? What—"

"Can't say exactly," he cut in, glancing over his shoulder at something she couldn't see. "But listen—what you did with The Heart? Making it a shared responsibility? Brilliant! Better than my original plan."

His image flickered. "Not much time. Just know… what's coming is bigger than Project Chimera and rooted deeper than the depths we knew existed."

"Let me help," Kara reached toward his image.

"You are helping. Every realm you unite makes what I'm doing possible." Pride shone in his eyes. "The Heart of Worlds isn't just a power source and a force of balance, Kara. It's a key. And when the Confluence comes—"

His image faded."Stay strong sister. Keep them united. And…" he grinned again, that familiar mischievous smile, "nice work with the Phoenix Merge. Though wait till you see what it can really do."

"Quin, wait!"

But he had faded, leaving the lingering warmth in her pendant and the certainty that somewhere, somehow, her brother fought for something vital to them all.

Through her window, dragons painted victory runes in the evening sky while Wind Mages danced through their flame-script. Haven pulsed with life and hope. Whatever challenges lay ahead, they would face them together.

Scene 4: Tomorrow's Promise

Haven's highest spire caught the light of multiple setting suns, the crystal surface warm beneath Shukára as she watched the celebration winds dance through the evening skies.

She sensed Zayn before she saw him—her energy called to him like lightning calling thunder. "Thinking deep thoughts?" he asked, moving to stand behind her. The air crackled between them, their powers reaching for each other.

"Quin appeared," she said, turning to face him. As Zayn's silver-blue eyes caught the fading light, she had to remember to breathe. The way he looked at her still sent electricity through her veins.

"And?" His hand found hers, power sparking where they touched.

"And the future's bigger than we thought." She stepped closer, drawn into his orbit. "Bigger than all of this."

His free hand traced the line of her jaw, leaving trails of storm-light on her skin. "We'll face it together."

When their lips met, reality rippled around them. Their powers merged without conscious thought, creating aurora lights that danced across Haven's evening sky. Dragons circling nearby roared in appreciation as the display rivaled their own flame-art.

Kara pulled back just enough to meet his gaze, their combined energy still swirling around them like a storm made of stars. "Now that war is over, let's stay in Haven together tonight."

His smile held both tenderness and heat lightning. "Every night... But we need to do something about those auroras!" Their shared laughter sent ripples of light through the evening sky.

As darkness fell, Kara and Zayn painted Haven's skies with new constellations—a promise of light, of love, of powers yet to be discovered. Whatever tomorrow might bring, they would meet it as one.